MOON

Denise sat _____
turned to face _____
night. I hope you don't think I was being—
well, too *direct* about you and Cara."

Joe laughed. "Not at all. We had fun for a
while, but she's not my type. We're through."
Joe pulled Denise a little closer. "Does that
answer the question you didn't ask?"

Denise blushed. "I just like to know how
things stand. It's always better to have as
much information as possible when you're
deciding what to think about something—or
someone."

"So what *do* you think?" Joe whispered
in her ear.

"I'm sure you know," Denise whispered
back. She looked up at him, taking in his
warm smile and sweet, friendly eyes. And
when he leaned over and kissed her—
tenderly, meaningfully, perfectly—she closed
her eyes, not wanting to disturb the deliciousness of the moment.

Bantam titles in the Sweet Dreams series. Ask your bookseller for titles you have missed:

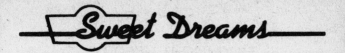

MOONLIGHT MELODY

Alicyn Watts

BANTAM BOOKS
NEW YORK • TORONTO • LONDON • SYDNEY • AUCKLAND

MOONLIGHT MELODY
A BANTAM BOOK 0 553 29985 9

First publication in Great Britain

PRINTING HISTORY
Bantam edition published 1994

Cover photo by Pat Hill

Bantam Books are published by Transworld Publishers Ltd, 61–63 Uxbridge Road, Ealing, London W5 5SA, in Australia by Transworld Publishers (Australia) Pty Ltd, 15–25 Helles Avenue, Moorebank, NSW 2170, and in New Zealand by Transworld Publishers (NZ) Ltd, 3 William Pickering Drive, Albany, Auckland.

Printed and bound in Great Britain by Cox & Wyman Ltd, Reading, Berkshire.

MOONLIGHT
MELODY

Chapter One

"Ah, freedom!"

Denise Reynolds took a deep breath of tangy salt air and bounded down her front steps, heading out for a morning run. In her emerald Lycra shorts and tank top and her wild brown hair pulled back with a tie-dyed scarf, Denise was an arresting sight.

It was early—just seven o'clock—on the first day of summer vacation. The grass was still damp with dew, and Denise swore she could actually smell the perfect sunshine. She had been looking forward to this morning ever since last September, and she intended to savor every moment of it.

Denise trotted down the street leading to the beach four blocks away. Scrambling over the sea wall, she set her sights on the mile-long stretch of sand that bordered Green Hill Cove. It was a smooth, quiet beach, its gently rolling dunes peppered with occasional tufts of seagrass. At the far end, where the tiny Narrow River spilled into the ocean, were many large boulders whose mysterious nooks and crannies Denise had always loved to explore. Every time she ran on the beach, she remembered the endless hours she had spent as a child hiding out among the rocks, capturing tiny hermit crabs and relocating them to new "homes" in the shallow tide pools.

Denise loved the early morning hours, before beachgoers arrived with radios and squealing children chased each other in and out of the surf. The only sounds that broke the peaceful silence were the waves on the shore, the mewing of sea gulls, and occasionally the faint voices of fishermen in a distant boat. Today there was no one to be seen except for a couple of men raking the sand far down the beach. Picking up speed, Denise settled into her regular stride.

Denise couldn't help but grin. Her head was filled with visions of a fabulous summer, complete with a fun, well-paying job, and all her days free for lazing on the beach with her friends. She could hardly believe how much had happened in just two short weeks!

One Tuesday afternoon after school Denise was wandering the halls of Green Hill High looking for her friend Laurel Bentley when she happened to walk by the music room. Vocal auditions were being held there for Blue Moon, a popular fifties band made up of teenage musicians and singers.

Denise peeked in and spied Mr. Browne, her former biology teacher and the manager of Blue Moon. He caught her eye and waved her in. Denise slipped inside and tiptoed around the edge of the room until she reached the place where Mr. Browne was sitting. He had smooth olive skin and piercing black eyes, and though Denise had always liked him, she found him a little intimidating.

A short, skinny boy was singing an off-key version of a Chubby Checker tune, accompanied by Blue Moon's keyboard player, Artie Smith. The boy was dressed in stiff blue jeans, black high-top sneakers, and a black leather vest several sizes too big. His bright red hair was slicked back and greased to a frightful sheen. Denise guessed he was trying for the James Dean look, but somehow it wasn't working.

When the boy had finished, Mr. Browne thanked him and promised to call him by Friday. Then he turned to Denise. "Well, Miss Reynolds, there's nobody else here, so I guess it's your turn," he said wearily. "I remember seeing you in a couple of talent shows here at school—what are you going to sing for us today?"

Denise's jaw dropped. "Oh, I—I'm not going to audition," she stammered. "I was just passing by, looking for Laurel, and—"

"But you *do* sing, don't you?" Mr. Browne interrupted.

"Well, yes," Denise admitted, "but that wasn't why . . ."

Mr. Browne sighed. "Come on, Denise, please don't be coy. What was that song you performed in the Spring Variety Show?"

"I really don't think I—" she began, but the teacher's glare cut her off in midsentence. "It was an old Frank Sinatra song, I guess," she said nervously.

"Go ask Artie if he knows it, then let's give a listen, okay?"

Mr. Browne started flipping through the papers on his clipboard while Denise talked with Artie. Almost before she knew what was happening, she was belting out a big-band number. At first she felt a little shaky, but by the time she finished the song, she was actually enjoying herself.

Mr. Browne smiled. "So, Denise. What are you doing this summer? I suppose you've got a job all lined up, right?"

"Not exactly," Denise admitted. "I applied for the job of recreation counselor at the playground, but I haven't heard from the Parks Department yet."

Mr. Browne's smile broadened. "Denise, I'm going to make you an offer you can't refuse. Four nights a week, your days will be free, really good money, and I guarantee you'll meet lots of guys. In case you haven't gotten the message, I want to hire you as my female lead singer. I've auditioned at least a dozen girls and not one of them is quite right. But I've got a good feeling about you. What do you say?"

Amazed, Denise sank into the nearest chair while she considered his offer. Artie had left and Mr. Browne was packing his papers into his briefcase when she finally spoke.

"If I take this job, I want you to know it has *nothing* to do with meeting guys," she said firmly.

"Denise, I don't really care why you take the job as long as you *want* to do it and to do it well. So are you in or out?"

"Well, I guess I'm in," Denise mumbled.

"Good!" Mr. Browne said briskly. "Your first rehearsal will be tomorrow night, seven o'clock at Artie's house. You know where he lives?"

Still dazed, Denise nodded.

"Okay. See you then." He started to leave, then turned back. "Congratulations, Denise. I think this is going to be one summer you'll never forget!"

Before Denise could thank him, Mr. Browne

6

walked out of the music room, leaving her alone with her whirling thoughts. It suddenly occurred to her that perhaps she should have discussed the situation with her mother before agreeing to take the job. But Mrs. Reynolds had always encouraged Denise and her older brother Mark to trust their own judgment. She also urged them to earn their spending money and to put something aside for college, so Denise and Mark had taken a wide variety of jobs over the past few years.

Last summer, Denise had worked as a baker's assistant in the early mornings and as a receptionist at a health club in the evenings. And every Tuesday and Thursday afternoon, she led the music club at the local retirement home. By the time school began in the fall, Denise didn't even have a suntan— she hadn't had time to go to the beach that was only a stone's throw from her front door. She had made her earnings goal, but she was bummed out all the same.

Denise decided that this summer would be different. It was actually going to seem like a real vacation for a change. Denise knew that Mr. Browne always had had the band booked solid at clubs, parties, and dances in town and up and down the coast. She would easily make as much money as she had last summer, maybe even more. She had a lot to look forward to—the beach, the sun, the gang, her morning runs, Blue Moon—who could ask for anything more?

As Denise passed the last lifeguard stand near the end of her first mile, she heard the sound of running steps on the sand behind her. She slowed down, hoping the other runner would simply overtake her and not interrupt her long-awaited Perfect Run on a Perfect Summer Day. But the steps slowed slightly to match her pace. *Oh, great,* Denise thought.

"Hey, how's it going?" a boy's voice asked as he came up along her right side.

Denise glanced over but couldn't immediately focus on his face because the sun was in her eyes. When her vision cleared, she saw a neon-yellow nylon visor, black sunglasses, and a nose covered with white zinc oxide. She didn't recognize the voice or what

8

little she could see of the face. She looked down to keep from being permanently blinded while she tried to figure out who was talking to her, and noticed that her uninvited companion was wearing the telltale orange shorts of the lifeguard team.

"I thought you guys didn't have to show up for work until eight-thirty," Denise grumbled.

"Well, good morning to you, too," the lifeguard said cheerfully. "I just wanted to get a good run in before the other guards turn up. Mind if I run with you?"

"I don't usually run with people I don't know. You could be some kind of health nut, or a psychopath, or you could ruin my pace or something."

He laughed, "Well, my name is Joe Ormand so now you know me. And I am *not* a psychopath. I'm a lifeguard."

"You can run with me if you want to—it's a free country after all. But I really don't like to talk while I run. It spoils the thinking part of it for me. I'm running six miles if you feel you're up to it."

"That's fine with me."

Joe settled into a solid—and silent—pace alongside Denise. After the third mile or so she almost forgot he was there.

As they neared the end of their sixth lap of the beach, they veered off toward the bathing pavilion, where Denise took a long, cold drink of water at the fountain. This was all a part of her summer running ritual, and she closed her eyes to enjoy it as she swallowed a final refreshing gulp. When she opened her eyes, she was looking straight at Joe Ormand, who was looking at *her* as if she were some kind of exotic creature in the zoo.

"What's the problem?" she asked, frowning.

"No problem," Joe answered. "You just seem to take your running a little too seriously. Jeez, it's summer, kid. Have fun! Live it up!"

"I *am* living it up," Denise said, a bit offended. "This is my idea of fun. And who are you to call me a kid? I'm going to be a junior at Green Hill High in the fall. What are you, a big senior?"

"Yeah, I just transferred to Randall High from Salem Day School," he said. "Listen, I'm sorry if I made you mad. It's just that

10

you seem so strict about your fun. You remind me of my old track coach. He got this strange, deep pleasure from running, too—I just wish I could get as much out of it as you both do."

Joe seemed sincere, but Denise wasn't sure if he was kidding her or not. Deciding to give him the benefit of the doubt, she reached out to shake hands. "Well, your coach was right, kid!" she said with a laugh. "I'm Denise Reynolds. I didn't mean to seem like such a witch—it's just that I'm used to having this place to myself in the morning."

"Well, I'm sorry I disturbed the peace. I'll come later from now on, okay?"

Denise really looked at him for the first time since they met, taking in his freckled, suntanned face, his friendly smile, and sparkling hazel eyes. "Oh, you don't have to do that," she said quickly. "I don't mind running with someone, but I really can't stand to talk or anything—I wasn't kidding about that. I'd love to run with you when you can make it."

"Great. I'll make it for sure. So, do you run for your school or just for fun?"

11

"I run cross-country at school," Denise answered. "I'm not one of the best on the team, though. I guess I don't have enough killer competitiveness to end up at the state championships. But I do enjoy the team stuff, and there's nothing like a good run on a crisp fall day."

"You really know how to make it sound appealing," Joe said. "Listen, I've got to get out of here. I've got some stuff to do before the gates open. I guess I'll see you tomorrow morning."

Denise laughed. "You'll see me way before then. My whole crowd comes to the beach every sunny day, and this year I'll be coming, too. You won't be able to miss us—ask anybody. I guarantee you'll be sick of us by the end of the summer."

"I guess we'll just have to wait and see, won't we?" Joe said, grinning. He waved and jogged off toward the lifeguards' office.

As Denise walked home, she wondered idly whether Joe Ormand might possibly be a new ingredient in her recipe for a perfect summer.

Get real, she told herself. *He seems nice*

enough, and maybe he's even cute under all that stuff on his face. But I've got enough going on as it is—the last thing I need is to get interested in some guy who probably won't give me a second thought. To remind herself of all her obligations and commitments to the band, Denise went over her summer agenda carefully. But for some reason, Joe's friendly, freckly face kept popping into her thoughts.

Chapter Two

Later that day, when Denise heard a knock at the kitchen door, she grabbed her beach bag and ran out of the house. Leaping from the porch, she noticed the familiar startled expression of her friend before she landed in a heap, taking Laurel down with her.

"Laurel, are you all right?" Denise cried. "I can't *believe* I did that!"

"Why not? You do it all the time. You always come out of your house like you're jumping out of an airplane. I swear, Denise, sometimes I think you're a crazy person," Laurel said as she picked the gravel from her knees. "I don't know if I can stand it much longer."

"Of course you'll stand it, Laurel, because you are the dearest, smartest, best friend in the whole world." They walked down the path to the sidewalk and headed for the beach. "Now tell me you're not."

Denise was a full six inches taller than Laurel, who was a perky, dark pixie type. Both girls wore what they thought of as their summer uniform—T-shirts and denim cutoff shorts over their swimsuits.

Laurel made a face. "If I'm your best friend, why do you keep trying to break every bone in my body? You have *got* to be more careful, Denise."

"Oh, I'll certainly try. I know how concerned you are about having any bruises or flaws that might harm your chances with Billy Keene, lifeguard extraordinaire."

Laurel sighed. "I have *no* designs whatsoever on Billy Keene! He's got that typical lifeguard attitude that I can't stand—you know, 'I'm the blondest, tannest, machoest guy on the beach, haven't you noticed?' Anyway, he appears to be dating Cara Smithson."

16

"Not that *you* noticed, right?" Denise joked.

The girls hopped over the seawall and made their way down the few craggy boulders that served as makeshift steps to the beach.

Denise and Laurel headed up the sand to the spot where their friends were already arranging their bags and blankets and towels and coolers. When they reached the group, Denise immediately began reorganizing the blankets to form a neat rectangle, creating what she called "Maximum Usable Beach Space."

Evan White groaned from his new blanket location. "Oh, Denise, how would we ever get along without you?" Evan was tall and lanky, with a mop of thick black hair and a perpetual crooked smile on his face. "Just when we're starting to recover from having our seats in the cafeteria reorganized every day of the school year, you're doing your 'Denise thing' on the beach!"

"Yeah, I know what you mean," Marcia Mead chimed in. Strangely, Marcia was a mirror image of Evan, minus about five inches in height. They seemed to have been

17

dating each other forever. "I was kind of hoping for a little break from being 'Denised' myself," Marcia added.

"No such luck, kids," Denise cheerfully retorted. "You can complain all you like, but in your heart of hearts, you have to admit that this group would just fall apart without my fond attentions."

"Maybe so," Kevin Dobbs said, "but why do we want to run screaming when we see you heading our way?" Kevin had been Denise's chem lab partner last year. He had quiet good looks and a lean athletic build. A lot of girls had secret crushes on him, but Denise and Kevin had always been "just friends."

"Well, thank you all *so* very much for those kind greetings," Denise joked as she secured the four corners of her own blanket with her sneakers and Laurel's sandals.

After she had applied her sunscreen, she sprawled flat on her back on the blanket. "I do not want to be disturbed," Denise called out. "There will be serious tanning going on here today."

"Uh, not yet, I'm afraid."

Denise sat up, squinting in the direction of the voice and trying to identify the body blocking her sun. It was Joe Ormand, and he looked uncomfortable.

"Oh, it's you again!" Denise said brightly. "I told you you'd see me before tomorrow. These are my friends." Denise waved in the direction of her group. "You guys, this is Joe Ormand, a new lifeguard in town."

"Uh—hi, everyone," Joe mumbled. "Denise, I'm sorry but you and your friends here are going to have to come up to the manager's office with me. You—uh—you're not allowed to access the beach by way of the seawall," he said sheepishly, as if reciting the regulation from memory.

Denise sat up straight. "So you're turning us in? Now that's an interesting way to make friends! Let's be sure to invite this guy to our next party," she said to the others with mock sarcasm, as they all hissed.

"I really am sorry about this, Denise, but you do have to come to the office with me," Joe said in his rules-and-regulations tone. Lowering his voice, he added, "Look, I'm not the one who saw you come over the seawall.

19

The beach manager did—he told me to come get you."

With a sigh of resignation, Denise jumped up from the blanket and began to pull on her shorts. "Don't worry about it, Joe. Although I must say this day is *not* turning out to be as terrific as I hoped it would be—and *you* keep turning up as the spoiler, mister!" She poked her finger at Joe's bare chest for emphasis, giving him a warm smile so he would know she was only kidding.

As Denise and Laurel headed for the pavilion, Laurel said, "I can't *believe* this! First day of summer vacation and you've already got us in the doghouse. Not only that, but you've also met the only new guy to come to this beach in years and you failed to mention it to me. On top of everything else, he's cute *and* he's a lifeguard. Was this some kind of little secret of yours?"

"Oh, Laurel, you know I don't care about lifeguards. I just met Joe this morning when I was running on the beach. And he's not all *that* cute."

"Hmmm—maybe I better start running on

the beach," Laurel mused aloud. "So you're not interested in him?"

"Well, I guess he *might* be my idea of an okay kind of guy," Denise hedged, purposely not looking at her friend.

"That's high praise coming from you," Laurel teased. "What are you going to do about it? Do you have a plan in mind?"

"Of course I don't have a plan. You know I'm not like that," Denise insisted.

"True," Laurel agreed. "You're the queen of organizing everything but your own love life. How can I help?"

"You can't!" Denise exclaimed. "Don't you dare say anything to *anyone* about this, especially to Joe Ormand! You know I can't stand being fixed up."

"Maybe if you let me plant a tiny seed, a romance will grow all by itself."

Laurel was getting under Denise's skin now, as only a best friend can. "No seed planting, do you understand me?" Denise yelled. "I mean it!"

"Okay, okay! Just kidding!"

When the girls reached the beach administration office, Mr. Chadwick, the beach manager, was not there.

"Oh, great. We're missing all this prime tanning time while Mr. Chadwick is sipping iced tea on the boardwalk or something," Denise griped. "Let's go find him."

She spun around just as Mr. Chadwick turned the corner on the way to his office. Denise didn't see him and slammed into him full force. Mr. Chadwick's glasses flew off and landed on the ground.

His face grew red as he struggled for words. "Denise Reynolds, don't you ever watch where you're going?" he hollered.

Denise, a little stunned herself, hurriedly picked up the glasses and handed them to him. "I'm sorry, Mr. Chadwick. We were just on our way to look for you."

"Denise, you know that I spend most of every single day sitting at that desk in that office. You also know that if I'm *not* there, I'll be back in a few moments," he fumed.

"I'm really sorry, sir," Denise said in her most apologetic voice. "Your glasses don't seem to be broken."

"Lucky for you, young lady," Mr. Chadwick

said, examining his eyeglasses carefully. "Well, Miss Hit-and-Run, I guess we'd better discuss your refusal to follow beach rules," he said, adjusting his glasses on his nose. He glared at Denise and Laurel and waved grandly in the direction of his dark cubbyhole. "Please step into my office, ladies."

Denise and Laurel settled into their chairs and immediately tuned out as Mr. Chadwick began his respect-for-the-rules speech. Laurel was looking at her nails, while Denise's blank expression hid a mind absorbed in thoughts of Joe Ormand.

Almost as if Denise had willed him to be there, Joe was waiting for the girls outside Mr. Chadwick's office when their lecture ended. Laurel immediately went off to the Snack Shack, leaving Denise alone with him.

Joe shrugged his shoulders helplessly. "I'm really sorry about that. It's just that I'm the newest guy on staff here so I guess I get to do the dirty work."

Denise laughed as they walked out onto the beach. "It's okay. It's not as if I haven't had hundreds of those little talks with Mr. Chadwick over the years. Let's see, there

23

was the one about water balloons and squirt guns not being allowed at the beach club, and an occasional scolding for sneaking my dog on the beach before it closed for the day—you get the picture. It's no big deal."

Joe smiled at Denise and raised his eyebrows quizzically. "Well, I hope you won't be too bummed about going to the lifeguards' barbecue with me tonight at Fisherman's Park—I mean, just to make peace. I don't want you to think I'm a total jerk."

Denise stared at him. *Is he actually asking me for a date?* she wondered. She decided to play it cool. "Normally I'd say sure, but it turns out I'm working at that barbecue. I sing with Blue Moon, the band that's playing for you guys tonight," Denise explained. "So I'll definitely see you there, but I probably won't get a chance to hang out with you much."

"How about doing something tomorrow night then . . . maybe the movies?" Joe asked.

Now *this* was definitely a date! Denise caught her breath and tried to sound casual as she said, "I'd love to."

Joe looked pleased. "Terrific. We can get something to eat afterward, if that's okay."

"Great, but—" Denise stopped short and turned pink, realizing that they were suddenly standing next to her blanket. All of her friends were following the last bit of conversation between her and Joe with great interest.

"Uh, I'll talk to you about it later," she said weakly. Joe nodded and waved, then ran down the beach toward his lifeguard station.

Her friends all laughed. "Hey, Denise, isn't that fraternizing with the enemy?" Evan chided.

Denise flopped down on her blanket and put her towel over her face. "I don't want to hear another word out of *anyone* about this!"

She lay there like that for a while, going over again and again in her mind what an amazing day it had been. She had met Joe Ormand that morning and he had asked her out already!

Chapter Three

That night, Denise stood in front of the full-length mirror in her bedroom, making final adjustments to her Blue Moon getup. The room was a vision in red and white—red-and-white-striped wallpaper, white furniture, red pillows, lamps, and rugs. Laurel always said it reminded her of a circus tent and made her head spin every time she walked in, but Denise loved it.

The members of Blue Moon were required to wear authentic fifties garb, so Denise had made a raid on every thrift shop in town. She had found a fantastic lavender circle skirt. It was so full that sometimes when she was practicing the Bunny Hop, she was afraid the swirling fabric might actually knock her over. She'd also bought a snug, ivory-colored short-sleeved sweater and a sheer lavender scarf. Anklets and saddle shoes were the finishing touch to her outfit.

But Denise was having trouble with her makeup. Her natural coloring was so vivid that she usually wore little more than a touch of lipstick. But Mr. Browne had told her to load on the makeup for Blue Moon's gigs because otherwise the spotlight would wash out her features. So she rummaged through her mother's makeup bags for foundation, eye shadow, eyeliner, and bright red lipstick.

As Denise applied a slightly shaky streak of liner around each eye, she wished she had it as easy as the boys in the band. At dress rehearsal the night before, Jay and Mike, the two male singers, had turned up in nearly identical outfits of jeans, T-shirts, and black leather jackets. And the rest of the band wore pretty much whatever they wanted.

Taking one last look at the stranger in the

mirror, Denise worried for a moment that when Joe saw her looking like this, he'd have second thoughts about their movie date. Then she laughed out loud, remembering Joe's weird appearance on the beach that day. If a guy who wore gobs of clownish white zinc oxide on his nose and cheeks to work gave her grief about the glop on her face, he'd be asking for trouble!

Driving to the beach a short while later, Denise was excited about seeing Joe that night and maybe showing off a bit as she sang. She might even have a chance to dance with him—Mr. Browne had said that band members who weren't performing in a number usually went out into the audience to get people dancing. Surely she'd hook up with Joe at some point.

When Denise first saw the platform that had been set up as Blue Moon's bandstand, she sucked in her breath sharply. The performing part of this little adventure was suddenly very real. Though the band wasn't due to begin playing for another twenty minutes, people were already starting to gather on the beach and boardwalk area set aside for dancing. The sun had not quite set, so the scene was lit by that wonderful opaque light of a summer evening. The food and drink stations were nearly ready to go—burgers were on the grill and sodas were on ice. As more people drifted onto the beach, Denise started to shiver. Though the songs had been perfected over what seemed like a thousand rehearsals, singing them in front of an audience—including Joe Ormand—was quite another story.

But when the performance actually began, Denise became so caught up in the music that she forgot all about the audience. She didn't have time to panic, or to join anyone for a dance. When she finally made it off-stage during the band's first break, Denise was in such a rush to get a cold drink that she would have passed right by where Joe was standing if he hadn't reached out to take her hand.

"Hey, Denise, you're doing a great job! You guys are really cooking up there," he said, smiling at her. Denise felt a rush of pleasure at his compliment. She thought Joe looked great in a crisp white polo shirt and jeans.

"Thanks," she said, smiling, too. "The songs are pretty fun, but those lights are really hot, and all that dancing around we do makes it worse. I feel as if I've just spent an hour in the steam room!"

"Denise, do you know Cara Smithson?" Joe asked, motioning to the girl who suddenly materialized at his side.

Denise's heart took an abrupt nosedive. "Oh, yeah. Hi, Cara," she said. Denise knew Cara slightly from school, and she and Laurel agreed that Cara was just too perfect to be real. Her clothes were always perfectly matched, her skin was always perfectly clear, and her shiny brown hair was always perfectly styled. Tonight she again looked perfect, in a peach sleeveless blouse that showed off her perfect tan, and white jeans that emphasized her perfect figure.

In contrast, Denise realized that she was soaked with sweat, strands of damp hair were escaping from her ponytail, and her makeup felt like it was melting. Thinking what a wreck she must look, she glanced from Cara to Joe. "So—uh—are you two here together?" she asked.

"Oh, no," Joe replied quickly. "Cara's here with Billy—you know, Billy Keene."

"Yeah," Cara said with a smile that revealed two perfect dimples. "And I think I'd better go find him before some other girl latches on to him. Nice seeing you, Denise. I had no idea you could sing like that."

"Thanks, Cara. I hope you find Billy . . ." Denise said, but Cara was already gone, swallowed up by the crowd. Turning back to Joe, she saw that he was grinning. "What's so funny?" she demanded.

"You. You don't beat around the bush, do you? About Cara and me, I mean."

Denise could feel herself blushing under the layers of makeup. "Well, I was just asking. Especially since I suddenly remembered Cara going on and on in chemistry last year about her boyfriend at Salem Day. I guess that was you, right?"

"Yeah, I guess it was. Cara and I went together for almost a year, but we broke up months ago. As soon as Billy Keene started paying attention to her, she seemed to lose interest in me."

Denise peered at Joe in that dim light, wondering how he felt about that.

He seemed to read her mind, because he smiled and said, "Oh, I'm not wrecked about it or anything. Cara's a nice girl, but I know when I'm outclassed. She suddenly developed this avid interest in muscles, and unfortunately, the only significant muscles I've got are in my head."

"Those are the best kind of muscles. Brawn can't compare with brains," Denise said.

Joe pretended to be offended. "Gee, thanks, Denise, but I don't think I'm *that* scrawny!"

"I didn't mean you were scrawny," she said, laughing. "*You're* the one who said—"

Just then Denise noticed Mr. Browne signaling the band to return to the stage. "Uh-oh—I've got to get back to work. If I don't get to talk to you again tonight, I guess I'll see you in the morning." She ran off before Joe could reply.

Back onstage, Denise couldn't help thinking about the way Joe had described his breakup with Cara Smithson. *Did he seem wistful?* she wondered. She looked out at the

crowd but couldn't see Joe or Cara anywhere. *So do I let this bug me or do I forget
about it?* Denise asked herself.

Mr. Browne answered her question for her
by snapping his fingers furiously from the
side of the stage, reminding her that she had
almost missed her cue. She shook the whole
thing off for the moment, and threw herself
into a soulful version of "Will You Love Me
Tomorrow?" Three songs later, while doo-
wopping behind one of Jay's songs, Denise
noticed that Cara and Joe were dancing
together.

*It's no big deal—they're just dancing, and
it isn't even a slow dance,* she told herself.
*But where's Billy Keene? Shouldn't he be po-
licing this situation?*

Quickly scanning the crowd, Denise saw
Billy deep in conversation with another lifeguard, not very far away from where Cara
was dancing with Joe. *Well, I guess if it
doesn't bother Billy, it shouldn't bother me,*
Denise thought, but she had to admit that
it did.

Twenty-five minutes later, the show was
over, and Denise was exhausted. She col-

lected her purse and headed in the direction of the parking lot. Since she hadn't seen Joe for some time, she assumed he'd left earlier.

Ten steps before she reached her car, however, Joe caught up with her. "You really were terrific tonight, Denise," he said. "You'd never know you weren't a fifties girl."

Smiling wearily, she said, "Thanks, but right now I feel like I'm fifty years old! This takes a lot out of me."

"Does that mean you won't be running tomorrow morning?" Joe asked. Denise thought he looked disappointed.

"Don't make any bets on it. I have a feeling I'll be sleeping in for a change," she said ruefully.

"Well, okay, just as long as you're all rested up by tomorrow night. Dinner and a movie, right? I can pick you up at seven."

Delighted that he seemed to be looking forward to their date, Denise said, "Absolutely. I live at the corner of Rudman and Beach streets, the yellow house. Maybe you could come by around six forty-five, so you can meet my mom and my dog . . . oh, and my gruesome brother."

35

"What's wrong with your brother?"

Denise laughed. "Oh, nothing really. He's actually a very smart and funny guy. But he worked so hard at his freshman college courses all year that he's kind of vegging out this summer. He slips into a television-induced coma and wears the same shirt day after day—it's not a pretty sight."

"Gee, I can't wait!" Joe said with a wry grin.

Denise opened the door of her red Volkswagen bug and folded herself into the driver's seat. "I have to go home now, or I'll fall asleep at the wheel. See you tomorrow, Joe."

He reached in the window and gently tugged her ponytail. "You bet you will. Six forty-five. I'll be there."

Denise watched him go, smiling dreamily. *Cara Smithson must be ancient history*, she thought. Then she caught a glimpse of herself in the rearview mirror and shook her head at the smudged, sweaty sight. *Good thing, too, because there's no way I could ever compete with someone that gorgeous!*

Chapter Four

Denise slept until noon the next day and spent the afternoon mowing the lawn and working in her mother's garden. Though she sometimes complained about these chores, actually she found them soothing, a welcome chance to think while she worked outdoors. By the time she had finished, it was late afternoon, and Denise wondered if she'd ever get rid of the day's accumulation of dirt from under her fingernails before her date with Joe.

By the time Joe's little blue pickup truck pulled up in front of Denise's house that evening, her manicure was impeccable. Dressed in a short khaki skirt and a French sailor's T-shirt, she finished buckling her blue leather sandals, bounded down the stairs, and opened the front door before Joe had started up the path from the gate.

As he stepped into the living room of the Reynolds' Cape Cod–style house, Joe looked around. Denise saw his gaze focus on a photograph that was prominently displayed on one of the bookshelves. It had been taken last Halloween, showing Denise and her mother standing with their arms around each other, dressed in identical black stretch jumpsuits and black high heels, with whiskers painted on their faces. Next to them was a man dressed in a tuxedo and top hat.

Joe stepped closer to the photograph and peered at it for a moment.

"Those two cats have to be you and your mom," he said. "You look a lot alike. But who's the guy . . . your dad?"

"No, that's my brother, Mark," Denise replied. "Dad died when I was five years old. But Mom says that's just how he looked when she first met him." Smiling, she added, "She loves this picture because she says it's like looking through a prism of images of our family—she sees my dad in Mark, and as you mentioned, she and I look so much alike."

"You really do," Joe remarked. "It's sort of amazing how—"

At that moment, Mrs. Reynolds stepped into the room. Like Denise, she was tall, with bright green eyes. The main difference between them was that Mrs. Reynolds' auburn hair had long since been tamed. Dressed in jeans, a chambray shirt, and tennis shoes, she hardly looked old enough to have a teen-age daughter and a son in college.

She extended her hand to Joe. "I'm so glad to meet you, Joe. Denise tells me you're new in this area."

"Well, sort of," Joe replied. "My family used to live in Grove Harbor and I went to Salem Day School there. But we moved to Randall last month so I'll be going to Randall High in the fall."

"You don't sound very upset about it,"

Mrs. Reynolds said. "Most teenagers would throw a fit if they had to switch schools for their senior year."

Joe shrugged. "Oh, I don't love the idea, but I already have some friends around here, and Grove Harbor is only twenty-five minutes away. But frankly I was glad to leave Salem Day. I mean, an all-boys' school is okay when you're twelve or thirteen, but it gets pretty tiresome when you're my age."

Mrs. Reynolds laughed. "I'm sure it does! You've certainly come to the right place. There are two coed high schools within a few miles of each other. You'll make up for a lifetime without girls in Green Hill Cove."

"Gee, thanks, Mom. Just when I was feeling like I was special," Denise said wryly, giving her mother a hug.

"But you are, honey. You're one in a million!" She turned to Joe and added earnestly, "There really isn't anyone quite like Denise."

"I've already found that out, Mrs. Reynolds. That's why I'm here," Joe said with a grin.

"Okay, Mom, that's enough," Denise said. "If I don't break up this little party, you'll

40

probably start taking out embarrassing naked baby pictures of me!"

"Hmmm—I wonder where I put that album . . ." Mrs. Reynolds mused, then added quickly, "Just kidding! Nice meeting you, Joe . . ." she called out as Denise pulled her out of the room.

When Denise returned to the living room, Joe smiled and shook his head. "Wow! Your mom is something else."

Denise laughed. "Yes she is, isn't she? She's raised us herself so we're all real close—more like friends than anything else."

"What does she do? I mean, for a living?" Joe asked.

"Mom's a free-lance illustrator for lots of graphics shops and advertising agencies. She's really good and she's got plenty of regular clients. She works during the evenings in her office downstairs. And she volunteers at the Community Child Care Center most weekdays."

"*And* she's raised you two? I'm impressed."

"Well, don't be *too* impressed, at least not until you get a load of my brother," Denise joked.

"So, when do I get to meet this unusual brother?" Joe asked, looking around furtively.

"Not tonight—Mark actually took a shower this afternoon, put on a sort of clean shirt, and headed off to the bowling alley with a friend. Maybe next time."

Joe looked slightly relieved.

They both happened to look down at the same moment to see Denise's dog, Bibeau, a floppy mixed breed, trotting into the room. Making a beeline for Joe, she gazed up soulfully into his eyes. When he leaned down to pat her, she rolled over in ecstasy, all four paws waving in the air.

"Denise, is this dog starved for affection or what?" Joe asked.

Denise laughed. "Oh, no. Bibeau gets like this around guys for some reason—I guess you could say she's boy-crazy."

"Maybe she needs professional help. Or at least a real boyfriend," Joe offered.

"It's funny, she's not nearly as interested in boy dogs as she is in human boys. Maybe she was a teenage girl in another life," Denise said. "We better get out of here before she falls head over heels in love."

"Yeah, that's probably a good idea."

As they headed for the door, Bibeau followed at Joe's heels, tail wagging hopefully.

"Maybe next time, Bibeau," he said. "I'm sure Denise wouldn't mind if I took you out sometime for a romantic run on the beach."

"Oh, please, be my guest! I wouldn't want to stand in the way of two creatures meant for each other. But she'd be a pretty strange prom date, don't you think?" Denise joked.

They laughed as they left the house, taking a last look back at Bibeau, who peered from the living room window with a betrayed look on her face.

"That's pretty pathetic. How can you stand it?" Joe looked for a moment as if he was considering asking Bibeau to go to the movies with them.

"Don't take it personally. I promise you, two minutes after we leave, she'll be snoring on the couch, not giving you a second thought."

Joe pretended to be hurt. "You mean, I don't make a lasting impression?"

Denise playfully punched him in the arm. "Cheer up—I'm sure *I'll* remember you. Now let's hurry or we'll have to sit in the first row with our noses pressed up against the screen."

After the movies, Joe and Denise were both starving. They made their way over to the Shun Lee Palace for Chinese food, and ordered an appetizer platter, a chicken and a shrimp entrée, and frozen fruit punches piled high with cherries and pineapple, plastic swords, and little paper umbrellas. They talked about the movie while sipping their drinks and waiting for their food.

"I'm sorry," Denise complained, "but these sci-fi flicks get goofier and goofier every year. I'm as willing as the next person to—what's the phrase?—'suspend my disbelief' to enjoy a far-out story like that, but one more stupid alien movie and I may throw up."

"I know what you mean. But movies like *Venusian Raiders* reflect people's endless interest in anything extraterrestrial," Joe said. "Ever since Copernicus pointed out that the Earth wasn't the center of the universe, the human imagination has run wild."

Denise grinned. "Well, thank you, Dr. Ormand, for your position on this vital issue! But what I really want to know is, how many ridiculous forms does Hollywood expect us to believe the extraterrestrial can take? Film producers don't take an intellectual interest in aliens—it's purely commercial, and all at our expense."

"Well, nobody's *forcing* anybody to go to the movies. It's only at our expense because we choose to hand over our money for a ticket. So we're actually encouraging Hollywood to mine the galaxy for gold each time we go to this sort of movie. And may I remind you, *you* chose tonight's flick."

"True," Denise agreed sheepishly. "Well, then, I made a mistake. From now on I won't be going to any more phony films, and you shouldn't either!" She folded her arms across her chest emphatically.

Joe laughed. "Are you always so outspoken? I mean, your mom seems so easygoing. Where does all this come from?"

"Don't let Mom fool you with that laid-back manner of hers," Denise said. "She has very strong opinions about almost everything. She doesn't care what our opinion is on something, just so long as Mark and I *have* an opinion we can state without sounding like total idiots."

"You ought to go out for debating," Joe teased.

"Oh, I don't think so. You see, my problem is that I get too charged up about things. Once I decide how I feel about something, I become kind of overwhelmed by my opinion. I'd be a terrible debater—I'd lose my cool in a minute."

Just then the food arrived and nothing mattered as much to either of them as eating. Denise finished first. Sitting back in her chair, she groaned. "I think I'm going to explode!"

"You know, Denise, you eat like you run— kind of purposefully, like there's a finish line you're headed toward that only you can see," Joe said.

"Well, thank you, Joe—I think," she said with a puzzled frown.

"Hey, I really admire you for it. I'm not kidding," Joe said earnestly.

Denise decided to change the subject. "So what's your story? I mean, you must have a life beyond lifeguarding."

"Sure I do—deep-sea diving, bungee-jumping, and tae kwon do classes keep me pretty busy," Joe joked. "Seriously, I'm not a very complicated guy. I was on the swim team at Salem Day, I run, and I like to read. I get pretty good grades, but I have to work for them."

"What about home?" Denise probed. "How many Ormands are there?"

"Three—me, Mom, and Dad. My dad designs boats in Grove Harbor, and Mom keeps the books for his business. That's about it. We lead pretty quiet lives," Joe said.

"That sounds nice. Life at my house is *never* quiet, not even when we're sleeping. My brother snores like you wouldn't believe!" Denise giggled.

Joe looked at her for a long moment, his expression suddenly serious. "You know, I have a funny feeling about you, Denise Reynolds. I've never met anyone quite like you. Everything about you is so distinct and clear—I really like that."

Denise looked down into her lap, unsure of how to respond. Joe reached across the table and lifted her chin up so he could look directly into her eyes. "What? Suddenly you've got nothing to say? I don't believe it!" he teased.

Feeling oddly flustered, Denise said softly, "That's one of the nicest things anyone has ever said to me. I—I guess I'm just not used to that sort of compliment." Taking his hand, she looked down at his palm. "Hey, you've got a great life line, and a really strong fate line . . ."

"Come on, Denise. Don't change the subject." Joe's fingers closed around hers. "You must have plenty of admirers. You're gorgeous, you're funny, and you're very talented."

"I guess I've always felt I'm a little, um, too much for most people." Denise looked down at their clasped hands. "You know, nothing about me is exactly average. I don't just have hair; I have a wild mop of something that *resembles* hair. I've always been the tallest girl in my class. I don't seem to be able to think about something quietly; in spite of myself, somewhere along the line I end up shooting off my mouth about it. I sense that a lot of people—especially guys—don't know what to make of me."

Smiling, Joe said, "Denise, I definitely know what to make of you. Your mom's right—you truly are one of a kind. And I wouldn't have it any other way." He gave her hand a squeeze, then released it and picked up the fortune cookie on the side of Denise's plate. "Let's see what your future holds." Pulling the slip of paper out of the cookie, he pretended to read aloud: "You will become involved with a cool lifeguard you recently met on the beach."

Denise laughed and reached for Joe's cookie. "It is dangerous to run with strangers."

Joe waved his arm as if to summon a waiter. "Sir, excuse me, but these fortune cookies are out-of-date. We need some that tell us stuff we don't already know!" he announced as Denise stifled a giggle.

The waiter rushed over to the table. "May I get you anything else?" he asked politely.

"Just the check, please," Joe answered with a wink at Denise.

* * *

The drive home was quiet, and when Joe
pulled up in front of Denise's house, he
turned off the ignition and turned to look at
her. "I wasn't just saying that stuff back at
the restaurant," he said, putting an arm
around her. "I really do think you're terrific.
I hope we can see a lot of each other this
summer."

"Me, too," Denise said happily. "This may
turn out to be the best summer ever." Then
she sat up straight and abruptly turned to
face Joe. "By the way, about last night. I
hope you don't think I was being—well, too
direct about you and Cara. Things like that
pop out of my mouth all the time."

Joe laughed. "Not at all. You're funny,
though. What would you have done if I'd said
'Oh, yeah, she's my date'?"

"I don't know," Denise admitted. "Nothing,
I guess. I mean, it's a free country. You can
go out with anyone you want."

"I *don't* want to go out with Cara Smithson. We had fun for a while, but she's not
my type. We're through." Joe pulled Denise

a little closer. "Does that answer the question you didn't ask?"

Denise blushed. "I hope you don't think I'm prying or anything. I just like to know how things stand. It's always better to have as much information as possible when you're deciding what to think about something—or somebody," she murmured.

"So what *do* you think, then?" Joe whispered in her ear.

"I'm sure you know," Denise whispered back. "What a funny thing, meeting each other like we did. What a nice twist of fate."

She looked up at Joe, taking in his warm smile and sweet, friendly eyes. And when he leaned over and kissed her—tenderly, meaningfully, perfectly—she closed her eyes, not wanting to disturb the deliciousness of the moment.

When their lips finally parted, Joe said, "I'm sure if you examine my palm again you'll see a very strong romance line. And if you look *real* close, you might even see us having a picnic supper tomorrow night at the jazz concert on the Town Green."

Smiling, Denise said, "That sounds perfect! Let's talk tomorrow and make plans. I've got to go in now—my mom and I have sort of a gentlewoman's agreement—as long as I'm in bed by midnight, she pretends she doesn't mind what time I got home. It works out pretty well." Denise opened her door, then turned back to give Joe a quick kiss on the cheek. "Thanks for a terrific night. I can't wait till tomorrow!"

She ran up the sidewalk and slipped into the house, watching from a window as Joe drove away. She closed her eyes and hugged herself, replaying that wonderful kiss over and over.

As she tiptoed up the stairs to her room, her brother Mark suddenly emerged from his own room into the shadowy hall like a ghoul from a crypt.

Denise let out a little shriek. "Mark! Why do you always *do* that?" She glared at her brother and shook her head. Mark had on a dingy white T-shirt and a pair of baggy Bermuda shorts that Denise figured hadn't been washed since last summer. And he had a bad case of "bed head," his hair all matted down on one side and sticking straight up on the other. Denise had to laugh. "One day, *one day,* I hope I can look as scary as you do and give you a taste of your own medicine," she added.

"Oh, you already have," Mark teased. "When you get all dolled up for your Blue Moon gigs—now *that's* scary." Mark chuckled and scuffed down the hall toward the bathroom, then turned back to say, "Oh, by the way, your Mr. Browne called tonight to remind you about practice tomorrow night. He said it was a 'don't miss' practice because you're going to be learning some new songs."

Denise whispered good night and closed the door of her room behind her. Then she threw herself on her bed, buried her face in her pillow, and screamed. She'd have to cancel her date for the jazz concert with Joe!

As she lay there, trying to think of some scheme to get out of the Blue Moon rehearsal, her mother came in to say good night. She sat down on the edge of Denise's bed. "So, what's the crisis of the moment? I *did* hear you scream, didn't I?"

"Oh, Mom, Joe and I had this perfect date

tonight and he invited me to go to the jazz concert tomorrow night with a picnic and everything and I came home to find out that there's a Blue Moon practice *tomorrow night*! This is a desperate situation. Do you have any ideas?" Denise looked at her mother pleadingly.

"Yes, I have an excellent idea," Mrs. Reynolds said. "Apologize to Joe, schedule another date, and go to your rehearsal because it is your job and it is the responsible thing to do." Her mom patted her on the shoulder. "See? It's not desperate at all—it's really very simple."

"Thanks a bunch, Mom," Denise said sourly. "This is just what I wanted to hear. You don't seem to understand that I don't *want* to go canceling dates on Joe Ormand! I really like him and I don't want him to slip away." *And back into the arms of Cara Smithson,* she thought to herself.

Mrs. Reynolds rolled her eyes in amusement. "Denise, Joe is not going to drop you if you can't go out with him tomorrow night. If he's as nice a guy as he seems, he'll understand your situation and be happy to make another date. If he isn't, it's better to find that out before you get in too deep. And another thing, a cardinal rule: Always keep your priorities in order, even when your emotions threaten to muddy up the picture. If you tend to your responsibilities first, you'll be surprised at how much it helps you keep the other stuff in perspective."

Denise heaved a sigh. "Oh, Mom, I know in my head that you're right. But my heart is pulling me in another direction—right in the direction of the Town Green tomorrow night."

"Well, honey, I'm not going to tell you what to do. But I *am* going to trust you to do the right thing. Let me know how it all turns out." She leaned over and kissed Denise on the forehead, then left the room.

Washing her face a few minutes later, Denise looked in the bathroom mirror and shook her head. *Oh, why couldn't I be working afternoons at the Bratmeister hot dog shop or something?* she thought. *I just can't tell Joe I won't be able to go. It would be different if I felt that this relationship was safely under way. As it is, I don't even know if he really likes me or if he just thinks I'm some kind of curiosity—especially compared to that dream girl Cara Smithson!*

After Denise crawled into bed, she lay there wide awake, trying to deal with her furiously conflicting feelings. But she knew perfectly well that, in the end, she had no choice. She'd cancel her date and go to the practice.

Chapter Five

The next day, Denise clambered over the rocks onto the beach and paused to squint into the early morning sun. She could see Joe waiting for her on the steps of the pavilion. She sighed and walked slowly over to him, wishing there was some way to avoid breaking the bad news.

Joe greeted her with a broad smile. "Hey, how ya doin'?"

"Oh, fabulous. Couldn't be better. Are you warmed up or do you need to stretch?" Denise asked. Maybe it would be easier to tell him once they were running side by side.

"I'm ready—let's go!"

They quickly settled into a comfortable pace and before long Denise was able to forget about her problem, at least for the moment. She enjoyed running with Joe in the quiet of the morning.

Denise broke the silence after they started the second mile. "I had a terrific time last night, Joe. It was really super."

"I had a great time, too," Joe said. "You're so easy to be with. It's like I've known you since kindergarten. But you know something weird? I had the craziest dreams all night! Huge paper umbrellas, dragons, aliens, you— it was like some kind of wild ride at Disney World!"

Denise laughed. "There must have been MSG in the food or something. I've heard that people can have strange reactions to it, but nothing like what you described. You're either a victim of your own active imagination, or else I made such an incredible first-date impression on you that I really blew your mind."

Joe chuckled. "Denise, you're a remarkable person, but I don't think even you could have caused these dreams!"

"I'll have to check and find out if it's happened to other guys I've gone out with," she teased. "You and I ate the same things, remember, and *I* didn't have strange dreams!"

They finished the rest of their run in silence, and as Joe took his turn at the water fountain, Denise knew she couldn't put off her announcement any longer.

"So, Joe," she said, "the bad news of the day is that I can't go to the concert with you tonight." She quickly looked at his face to judge his reaction. Strangely, there was none. "When I got home last night," she continued, "Mark gave me a message from my band manager about an important practice tonight. I'm really sorry, but it's my job. I—I hope we can go out another time," Denise added quickly. When Joe said nothing, she glared at him. "Gee, don't be so bummed out about it!"

Laughing, he put his arm around her in a quick hug. "Oh, Denise, of course I'm bummed out, you goof. I was just wondering if there's time to call my mom and tell her before she starts making the stuff for our picnic. She said she was going to bake these little gourmet chicken pies first thing this morning."

"Oh, no!" Denise wailed. "I'm *so* sorry! I should have called you last night to let you know, but it was late and I didn't know you'd be going to so much trouble . . ."

Joe smiled. "Are you kidding? Nothing's too much trouble for my official Second Date with Denise Reynolds. Anyway, it was my mom's idea. She loves having a chance to cook special stuff because these days she usually only gets to feed me and my dad cold sandwiches on the run."

"Call her *right now*," Denise urged. "I'll feel terrible if she's gotten all involved in cooking for nothing." Grabbing Joe's arm, she pulled him in the direction of the pay phone.

He started to dial his number but hung up after the first couple of digits. "You know what?" he said, tapping his head like he'd just had a brainstorm. "I'm going to let her go ahead and make those pies and fix up a nice picnic. And then I'm going to take *her* to the concert. My dad's been working a lot of nights lately, and I bet she'd be tickled if I asked her to go with me. She thinks I'm too embarrassed to do things with her, so she'll be extra surprised if I invite her."

Denise looked at him quizzically. "Why would she think that?"

"Oh, she's read all those 'Getting Along with Your Teenager' books and she's always convinced I'm going through some teenage phase or another. So she read somewhere that teenagers are embarrassed to be seen in public with their parents, and now she's careful not even to ask me to go to the grocery store or the library with her anymore."

Denise stared at Joe. "What would make her believe you're one of those surly, miserable kids she's read about? You're one of the most levelheaded guys I know."

Joe laughed. "I don't think she *really* thinks I'm like that. But I do think she's afraid that if she doesn't make all the right moves I'll turn into one. And because I'm an only child, she thinks she has just this one chance to get it right. It's made her a big believer in child development theories."

"Well, then I think it's a wonderful idea to take your mom to the concert. I wish it were me but since I can't go, I'm just as glad it's her." Denise took Joe's hand. "Do I get a rain check for the evening, though?"

Joe squeezed her hand in both of his. "Absolutely. When's your next night off?"

"Monday. Not the most romantic night of the week but I'm not in a position to be picky."

"I'll take it!" Joe said. "There's a clambake and reggae fest every Monday night at Fido's Fish Shack on Scarborough Beach. We're there!"

When Denise headed home, she was relieved. She was feeling happier than she had ever imagined she would be when she set out earlier that morning.

Won't Mom smirk when she finds out how right she was—again!

Shortly after nine o'clock that night, Denise threw her stuff into the backseat of her car, eager to hit the road. The Blue Moon rehearsal had gone well—they'd mastered three new songs and a couple of dance steps

62

in record time, so the band members had been let loose early. All she could think of was rushing downtown in time to catch the last bit of the jazz concert with Joe and his mom. *What a lucky creature I am,* she thought smugly. *That's what I get for doing the right thing!*

As Denise zipped along the ocean road, she had to pay close attention not to exceed the speed limit. When she got caught behind a slow-moving tow truck, she nearly had a fit. By the time she arrived in the area of the Town Green, she was almost hyperventilating, worrying about whether she'd find a parking spot, or even whether she'd find Joe and Mrs. Ormand at all. The jazz concerts were always well attended, and she'd have to do a lot of creeping around and peering at people's faces in the dark to locate them.

Finding a parking spot right off the green, Denise hoped it was a sign that she'd find Joe just as quickly. She hopped out of her car and made a beeline for the crowd sitting on the lawn listening to the concert.

The entire green was about the size of a city block, surrounded on three sides by old buildings—a church, the library, post office, and town hall—and on the fourth side by the ocean. Every few years it was flooded by the waves crashing over the seawall during a wild storm. The salt water would kill the grass, and it would take nearly a year for the green to be green again. Right now, however, the lawn was lush and the flower beds around the edges were crowded with colorful blossoms.

Denise scuttled around the edges of the crowd in sort of a half crouch, trying not to obscure anyone's view while she searched for Joe. By the time she had made her way from one side of the green to the other, her thigh muscles were burning from her strange crouch-walking and she still hadn't caught a glimpse of Joe and his mom.

I should have known better. It's impossible to find anyone in this crowd. I might as well give up. Oh, well, at least I tried, Denise thought as she stretched to get the kinks out of her legs. Before heading off in the direction of her car, she scanned the crowd one last time—and suddenly caught sight of a familiar fluorescent orange lifeguard jacket glowing faintly in the moonlight, right where Denise had begun her search. *This surely is my lucky night!* she thought, grinning as she ran in the direction of where she'd spotted Joe.

But as she approached the blanket, she stopped short and sucked in her breath sharply, still several feet from where Joe was sitting. Next to him on the blanket, attentive and serious and oh-so-music-loving, was someone who was definitely *not* his mother. Cara Smithson was sitting there, hugging her knees, listening soulfully with her head tilted slightly to one side, as if she were taking a final exam for a music appreciation course.

Denise just stood there staring, filled with disbelief and rage. It wasn't until many moments later, when the music had ended, the applause had died away, and the audience were beginning to gather their belongings and leave, that Denise was able to collect her wits. The very last thing she wanted was for that two-faced, double-dealing Joe Ormand to know she'd been there and seen him enjoying the concert with his "mother."

Denise turned and fled, but she couldn't even remember where her car was. Spying it suddenly, Denise ran to it, flung open the door, and got inside. She fastened her seat belt with trembling fingers, then sat staring straight ahead for what seemed a very long time, taking a series of deep breaths to control the pounding of her heart.

How ugly! Denise thought. *Joe Ormand is a liar and a cheat! I can't believe I fell for all those meaningful glances and sensitive words. I can't believe I believed him when he said Cara wasn't his type, and that they'd broken up for good. I feel so hurt and stupid, I could scream!*

But she didn't—her car windows were wide open, and she didn't want to make a scene. Instead, Denise gritted her teeth and banged the steering wheel with both fists until they ached. Then, still fuming, she started her car and began driving home.

I bet Joe and Cara had a good laugh about how gullible I was, she thought. *"It's a wonderful idea to take your mom to the concert," I said. Yeah, right! And I thought it was so sweet of him to think of asking her. How dumb can I be?*

A passing car honked, and Denise realized that she'd been driving without her headlights. She quickly turned them on.

Her eyes filled with sudden tears and her nose began to run, the way it always did when she started to cry. She groped in her jeans pocket for a tissue. Not finding one, she blinked hard and wiped her nose with the back of her hand.

Pulling up to the curb in front of her house, Denise sat there for a moment, trying to calm herself down before going in. *I guess this wasn't my lucky night after all,* she thought as she finally got out of the car and dragged herself up the path to the front door.

Chapter Six

The minute Denise opened her eyes the next morning, everything she'd seen and felt the night before came rushing back as if it had just happened. Taking a long, hard look at herself in the bathroom mirror, she shuddered. Crying too much and not sleeping enough had left her eyes red and swollen, and her hair was even more of a mess than usual.

Denise trudged toward the bed but stopped dully in front of her running shoes. *I know I should run,* she thought. *It would probably do me good.* She eyed her bed longingly, but

69

after five full minutes of internal debate, the runner in Denise won out. She put on her running gear and slipped out of the house. Unable to bear the thought of meeting Joe on the beach, Denise ran in the opposite direction to her school. She'd make laps around the outdoor track instead.

As ever, it didn't take long for the physical effort to begin its soothing effect on Denise. After her third mile, she felt calm enough to take a clearheaded look at the situation.

Joe may not be a complete heel, she reasoned. *He obviously misjudged how he felt about Cara, that's all. He must have fallen for her all over again, and Cara probably wants him back—she finally figured out that Billy Keene is an arrogant jerk. Well, it's a good thing I found out about them before I did something really dumb, like fall in love with Joe. Right again, Mom! I'm sure glad I've got that all straightened out.*

Having carefully analyzed Joe, Cara, and herself, Denise decided that she felt much better. That conviction lasted through the rest of her run, but on the way home, the hollow feeling in the pit of her stomach returned.

It may take a little longer than I thought to get over Joe, she admitted, *but I'm sure I won't feel like this forever. After I've seen him with Cara a few more times, I'll be completely cured. All I need is a little more time.*

When Laurel stopped by a few hours later on her way to the beach, Denise was strongly tempted to make some excuse not to go. But she knew that would be cowardly, and besides, she couldn't hide from Joe indefinitely. So she put on her suit, grabbed her beach bag, and went. If she ran into him, as she was bound to do, Denise was sure she could handle it. Surrounded by her friends, she'd *have* to handle it. She'd be casual and cool, but friendly in a distant kind of way.

Denise and Laurel were standing in line at the concession stand, waiting to buy cold drinks, when Joe sauntered over to them.

"Hi," he said cheerfully. Smiling at Denise, he asked, "How was your rehearsal last night?"

71

"Fine," she answered, not looking at him.

"Where were you this morning? I had to run all by myself—I was a little late so I guess you were finished by the time I got here."

"Oh, I ran at the school today," Denise responded, intently studying the menu next to the window of the concession stand.

"What's the matter? Did you need a break from me? Don't tell me we've been seeing too much of each other," Joe joked.

Denise didn't laugh. She didn't even smile. Laurel watched the exchange very carefully, her puzzled gaze finally focusing on Denise.

After a long, awkward silence, Joe cleared his throat and asked Denise whether it was okay if he called her that evening.

"Well, that would be kind of pointless," she answered icily. "Blue Moon's playing for the dance at the state beach so I won't be home." Although Denise was staring at the back of the girl ahead of her to avoid looking at Joe, out of the corner of her eye she saw him glance at Laurel and mouth "What's with her?"

Laurel shrugged. "Beats me," she mouthed back.

Denise couldn't stand it another minute. She excused herself, saying, "I'm not really very thirsty anymore," and rushed back to her blanket. Without a word to the rest of the gang, and before Laurel had time to catch up with her, Denise gathered her things and headed for home. "Handling" her situation with Joe was proving to be a lot harder than she'd imagined it would be.

Determined to get a grip on herself, Denise got dressed for a therapeutic trip to the Pier Mall. *There's nothing a little time in a dressing room and a little money in my pocket won't take care of,* she thought. But after a few hours of aimless, unenthusiastic window-shopping, and dozens of rejected sweaters, shorts, and even shoes, Denise returned home empty-handed except for a bottle of nail polish, and no less heartsore than when she had set out. She found three telephone messages, written in Mark's all but illegible scrawl. If she didn't know his handwriting so well, she would never have known that the messages read, "Laurel—Urgent."

Sighing at the prospect of the conversation she knew she was about to have, Denise called Laurel, who picked up the telephone on the first ring.

"I *knew* it was you, you lunatic! Now, what do you mean by acting like that to Joe?" Laurel bellowed without even saying hello. "That wasn't very endearing behavior."

Denise didn't reply.

"Denise, I'm not kidding. What's wrong with you anyway? Did something happen between you two? Or should I say, did something happen to *you*, because if something happened between the two of you, Joe would have been aware of it, and he obviously wasn't. Now let's hear it," Laurel demanded.

"It's a long story, Laurel, and I'm not sure I'm up to telling it right now," Denise responded wearily.

"Listen, Denise, this is the first really serious potential boyfriend you've had in over a year," Laurel lectured. "Joe's a great guy. Why are you freezing him out like this? There *must* be a reason!"

"Laurel, if you must know, Joe is getting back together with Cara Smithson. Even though he told me he's not interested in her, I saw them together at the jazz concert last night, after he said he was taking his *mother*! I just don't understand why he couldn't be honest with me. I feel so *stupid*!" she moaned.

"Oh, Denise, I'm so sorry. And here I've been thinking all day that *you* were screwing everything up. I feel just terrible. As for *him*, what a rat! How could he? First of all, Cara Smithson can't hold a candle to you. And then to go around asking you out, romancing you, and then sneaking around with that . . . that . . . that plastic female! Clearly Joe Ormand is a world-class jerk, just another one of those self-centered, empty-headed lifeguards we've despised all our lives! I'm really surprised at you, Denise. If something like that happened to me, I'd be screaming, throwing things, putting hexes on both of them!"

"Oh, come on, Laurel. It's just that, you know, what good would that do? I mean, it's not as if Joe and I were going steady or engaged to be married or anything. We were just starting to date, just getting to know each other. . . ." Denise swallowed hard, then added, "Or at least I *thought* I was getting to know him. Anyway, it's not against the law for a guy to change his mind, though I wish he hadn't lied to me."

She leaned against the wall, sliding down until she was sitting cross-legged on the floor. "And you know, Laurel, in spite of everything, I really don't think Joe's a total jerk. I don't exactly know what his problem is—I guess he just thought he'd gotten over Cara but now he's discovered he hasn't, and he doesn't have the guts to tell me about it."

"Well, aren't you being mature about this!" Laurel sputtered. "Like I said, I'd be going berserk!"

"I did at first, but now I just feel kind of sad because I really liked him. Mostly I guess I feel disappointed in Joe," Denise said. "I thought he was honest, and nice, and that he really liked *me*. But he wasn't and he didn't, so I'll just have to chalk it up to experience and forget about him."

"Anything I can do to help?" Laurel asked sympathetically.

After a moment's pause for thought, Denise said, "I wouldn't mind if you came with me to Blue Moon's gig tonight. It'll be nice to see a friendly face in the audience, and besides, you always take my mind off my troubles."

"*And* your homework, *and* your chores, *and . . .*"

Both girls laughed, then agreed that Denise would pick Laurel up at six-thirty so they could drive to the state beach together.

Denise spent the next few hours giving her room a thorough cleaning for the first time in months, reading magazines, and painting her nails a violent shade of red. All that activity helped to push Joe and Cara out of her thoughts, but not very far.

At about four-thirty, Denise heard her mother come into the house after a trip to the supermarket. A few minutes later, Mrs. Reynolds came upstairs. As she entered Denise's room, her eyes widened. "Good heavens! You've actually cleaned your room!" she exclaimed. "I must say I'm impressed."

She plopped down on the edge of Denise's bed. "So what else is going on? Oh, never mind—I can see for myself," she said as Denise waved her hands under her mother's nose. "Nice nails, Miss Dracula. Where did you ever find such a stunning shade? At the butcher shop?"

"Very funny, Mom. I went to the mall to poke around, and I was looking in the pharmacy for something to jazz up my Blue Moon makeup, but all I found was this nail polish."

"Who did you go with?" her mother asked. "Laurel?"

"No, I went by myself. I needed to be alone—I guess I was paying a visit to Dr. Mall."

Mrs. Reynolds raised her eyebrows. "Problems?"

With an elaborate shrug, Denise said, "Oh, nothing much. Just that everything's off—over, ended, kaput—with Joe Ormand." She threw herself on her bed and stared at the ceiling.

Her mother sat up straight, gazing at Denise in surprise. "How did that happen? The last I heard, everything was great."

After Denise had told her the whole story, Mrs. Reynolds shook her head sadly. "Well, that *is* pretty nasty, honey. I'm so sorry it turned out this way," she said.

"I just knew it, Mom! I told you that if I didn't go to the concert with Joe last night something would mess it all up." Denise could feel herself getting sad and mad all over again, and her eyes were starting to burn.

"Denise, listen to me," her mother said gently. "You must know that whether you went to the concert with Joe last night or not, this 'something' that 'messed it all up' was going to happen anyway. If he's still interested in Cara, and she's still fond of him, he was bound to end up getting back together with her sooner or later. Remember what I said before—it's better to get out of a difficult situation early on rather than waiting till you're emotionally in the thick of it. Think of how much worse you'd feel if you'd been going with him for months, even falling in love with him."

"That's what I tried to tell myself, Mom," Denise said. "But guess what? I was already in way over my head. I've never been as crazy about a boy as I was about Joe! I mean, I thought he was different, that he didn't think I was too weird, or too pushy, or too whatever, the way most guys do. But obviously I was wrong."

"I see." Mrs. Reynolds was silent for a moment. Then she said, "What did Joe have to say about all of this? I don't mean to pry, honey—I'm just curious as to how he explained his behavior."

Glaring at her mother, Denise said, "Mom, he *didn't* explain it. I don't *want* him to explain it. I'm already as humiliated as I can be. Why would I want to put myself through a whole conversation with him about it?" She resumed her long, hard stare at the ceiling.

Mrs. Reynolds stared at her. "You mean, you haven't discussed it with him? You've just decided that it's all over between you based on what you saw—or what you thought you saw?"

"I *know* what I saw, Mom, and it wasn't Joe and his mother!" Denise snapped. "It was Joe and Cara Smithson all cozied together on that blanket. I'd have to be *blind* not to have seen it!"

"But Denise, you said it was awfully dark— you could hardly see where you were going," her mother pointed out. "How can you be sure it was Cara? And even if it was, that doesn't necessarily mean they were on a date. Maybe Joe's mother couldn't make it, and he and Cara just happened to run into each other at the concert. They ended up sitting together, the way friends would normally do."

Denise groaned. "Trust me. It was her, all right. And besides, Cara's a professional girlfriend—she wouldn't know how to be 'just friends' with a guy if her life depended on it!"

"Well, it seems to me that until you have an actual conversation with Joe about what you saw, it's not fair to assume the worst."

Denise was getting upset. "Mom, do you have to be so reasonable about everything? Can't I just be really, really angry about this mess without wondering if I'm being fair to Joe or Cara? *I'm* not the one who went to the concert with someone else, remember!"

Mrs. Reynolds reached out and brushed

Denise's tousled hair off her forehead. "I'm sorry, honey. I know it must sound like I'm taking Joe's side. Really, though, I'm sticking up for you. I want you to consider the situation from every angle, try to make sense of it, for your own good."

"I think—for my own good—that I'll just stay far, far away from Joe Ormand," Denise declared. "I'm already miserable about this whole thing. I don't want to prolong the agony."

"That's just my point, Denise. I think you'll prolong the agony if you *don't* have a talk with Joe. You know that I usually don't interfere with your personal life or your brother's. But in this particular case, let me give you a word of motherly advice."

When Denise covered her ears with a pillow, Mrs. Reynolds just chuckled and raised her voice a notch. "Don't allow yourself to drown in a pool of self-pity and righteous indignation, honey. Take control of the situation. Face up to him and give him a chance to tell his side of the story. What he has to say may be a pleasant surprise. On the other hand, if he tells you that Cara's the girl for him, it will hurt a lot but at least you'll know where you stand."

Denise didn't respond. In spite of the pillow, she had heard every word her mother said, and though she knew it made sense, she had absolutely no intention of confronting Joe and requesting an explanation. She'd embarrassed herself enough by asking him about Cara the first time—he'd even laughed at her for being so obvious. Not only that, but since Joe apparently hadn't told Denise the truth then, he'd most likely lie to her again.

Mrs. Reynolds leaned over and kissed her cheek, then stood up, saying briskly, "Think about it, okay?"

No way, Denise thought emphatically as her mother left the room. *As far as I'm concerned, Joe Ormand is history!*

Chapter Seven

That night at the state beach, Denise looked out into the audience with huge, wide eyes. She'd heard Artie strike the familiar cue chord—twice, as a matter of fact. She knew she was supposed to sing something, but she didn't have the faintest idea what it was. No words would form, not in her mind, not in her mouth. All she could summon up were images of Joe—Joe kissing her in his truck, Joe running beside her in the sunlight at the beach, Joe sitting next to Cara Smithson in the moonlight at the concert. Her mind was so filled with these pictures that she couldn't seem to concentrate on anything else.

The people in the audience were beginning to fidget and cough. *I was just singing this song to myself two minutes ago. What's wrong with me?* Denise thought, panic-stricken. She was just trying to decide whether she should pretend to faint or run off the stage and hide when suddenly the words to the song flooded her memory all at once and she gave Artie a furtive signal to start again.

The next couple of songs went smoothly enough, with Jay and Mike standing a bit closer to Denise than usual. That gave her a little moral support, which helped, but she was still a little shaky. Fortunately, the crowd didn't seem to notice that she was having a problem—they were having too good a time. Everyone was dancing and laughing, making Blue Moon appear to be more of a backdrop to a good party than the featured performers in a show. This time, the platform stage was set up on the beach itself with the ocean directly behind it. The people danced on the broad boardwalk in front of the beach pavilion while onlookers leaned over the railings, enjoying the music and the cool, salty breeze.

After the first set of songs, Denise was looking forward to her break as if it were a long-awaited vacation. She walked off the stage and disappeared behind the band's equipment van to catch her breath.

"Just the person I was looking for." Mr. Browne's deep baritone startled her. "Are you having a little bit of trouble tonight? Anything I should know about?" He was glaring at Denise with his arms folded over his chest, and she remembered her freshman year, when she had first been warned about Mr. Browne's reputation as the wrong teacher to run into when you were wandering the hallways without a pass. He was strict but fair, and everyone tried to stay on the right side of him. Denise knew that tonight she was definitely on his wrong side.

"Oh, no sir, not at all," she said quickly. "I was just having a hard time remembering the start to that one song, that's all."

"Denise, you're performing nowhere near your potential tonight. Do I have to remind you that you are the lead singer of this group, and as such, you have to be on top of every song, every number, every time you walk out on that stage? How well you perform is the key to our success as a group. In other words, if you foul up, we're dead. Got it?"

"I—I know that, Mr. Browne," Denise faltered. "But I'm having a little trouble concentrating tonight. You see, I have—"

Mr. Browne cut her off. "Listen, Denise. This is not brain surgery we're doing here. And it's not like you're some big rock star who can afford to pull the prima donna routine. You're a kid, this is a fun job, and you should be having fun doing it. But you should also be taking it seriously enough to do it right. Do we understand each other?"

At a loss for words, Denise hung her head.

"Okay, Denise," he said with a sigh. "If there's some big problem I need to know about, you better tell me now. Because if you don't think you can continue performing with Blue Moon, I'm going to have to begin looking for a replacement right away."

Denise quickly looked up. "No, I'll be fine,

really. I'm sorry about tonight. I promise I'll do much better during the rest of the show. And I promise this won't happen again, sir."

"I hope not. You have got to get a grip on yourself and I mean immediately. You know the Davincis are in the audience tonight, trying to decide whether to hire us for their party at the Dunes Club. Don't blow it for us, okay?"

Denise gasped. She'd forgotten all about the Davincis. They were the wealthiest couple in town, and every summer they hosted a huge bash at the swankiest beach club on the coast. This could be Blue Moon's biggest gig of the season, and Denise knew perfectly well that tonight's performance could make or break the deal.

"Oh, my gosh, Mr. Browne. I *am* sorry," she said. "Don't worry. I'm fine and I'll be fine—I'll be *great*—for the rest of the show. We'll get the Davinci party, I'm sure of it!"

Mr. Browne patted her on the arm. He even smiled slightly. "That's more like it. Now let's get back to work, shall we?"

Denise followed his lean form around the

van back to the stage area, determined to do her very best. She got back onstage and belted and crooned her way through the next two sets of songs like a true professional, and the other kids in the group performed up to her level. Everything was smooth as silk until their second-to-last song, a wistful arrangement of "Tenderly."

Denise was working hard at it to begin with because it was one of their new numbers. Right in the middle, just when she'd built up to an emotional peak and was feeling really good about the song, she glanced out over the audience. Like a magnet, her gaze was drawn to two familiar faces. Joe Ormand and Laurel were leaning on the railing of the boardwalk, deep in conversation. Startled by the sight of Joe and stunned to see her best friend talking with him so chummily, Denise fumbled a lyric and lost the beat for a second. It was all she could do to regain her concentration and finish the song.

She closed her eyes tight for the next and final number, afraid that if she saw Laurel and Joe again, she'd have another amnesia attack. But when the song was over, Denise knew she'd have to open her eyes or look like a zombie while she and the other band members took their bows. Though she tried to avoid looking out into the audience, she couldn't help it, and saw Joe and Laurel again out of the corner of her eye. They were smiling and applauding like mad, just as if nothing was wrong.

And then Denise saw something that really blew her mind. Just beyond Joe was none other than Cara Smithson.

This has to be some kind of recurring nightmare, she thought. *It's bad enough for those two to be carrying on together, but do they have to keep doing it right under my nose? Don't they have anywhere else to go?* What made it even worse was that Laurel seemed to think it was perfectly okay.

Feeling sick, furious, and betrayed, Denise stormed offstage even before the clapping had ended. Ignoring the startled glances from the rest of the band, she snatched up her purse and raced to the parking lot. She had to get out of there fast before she hurt someone—Joe, Cara, Laurel, she didn't care who.

Half a mile down the ocean road, Denise suddenly remembered that Laurel would be counting on her for a ride back to town. She slowed down automatically, about to turn around and return to the beach. Then her eyes narrowed. *Let Laurel catch a ride with her new best friends, Joe and Cara,* she thought angrily. *Those three traitors deserve each other!*

But by the time Denise reached home, she was feeling more than a little guilty about leaving Laurel behind. *Well, it's her own fault,* she told herself as she trudged up the path to her front door. *Laurel made her choice. She abandoned me, so I had a perfect right to abandon her, so there!*

Denise hurried upstairs, grateful that she hadn't run into either her mother or Mark. But her steps slowed as she approached her bedroom. The door was ajar, and a light was on. When Denise walked in, her heart sank. Her mother was sitting in the easy chair, and she wasn't smiling.

Uh-oh, Denise thought. *Just what I need—another dose of motherly advice.* But aloud she said, "Hi, Mom. What's up? Do you want me for something?"

"Yes, Denise. I do. As a matter of fact, I want an explanation, and it had better be good," Mrs. Reynolds said evenly. "Why did you leave Laurel to find her own way home from the beach? She phoned a few minutes ago from the parking lot, wondering if I had heard from you. Not only was I afraid something had happened to you but I was also worried about Laurel, stranded out there without a ride."

Avoiding her mother's eyes, Denise walked over to her dressing table and began taking off her rhinestone earrings.

"I'm waiting, Denise," her mother said. "What's the story here?"

Denise sank down onto the dressing table bench. "Joe and Cara were there tonight, and Laurel was hanging out with them like they were all old pals or something. I mean, I almost threw up right there onstage! I was so mad that all I wanted to do was get away as fast as I could, and by the time I remembered Laurel—well, I figured she'd probably ride home with them."

"You were wrong," Mrs. Reynolds said sharply. "Imagine how you'd feel if you were in Laurel's position, Denise. She didn't try to get a ride because she naturally assumed she'd be driving home with you. Laurel told me on the phone that she was going to call her mother and ask to be picked up, which means that she had to wait all alone in the parking lot until Mrs. Bentley got there. No matter how upset you were, taking off like that was an extremely thoughtless and irresponsible thing to do, Denise."

Denise stared down at her saddle shoes. "I know," she mumbled. "I just wasn't thinking straight, I guess. I'll call Laurel in a few minutes and apologize."

"Honey, you really need to get a grip on yourself about this Joe thing," her mother said in a gentler tone. "It's not like you to get all bent out of shape like this over a boy."

"I know," Denise said again, "but I can't seem to help it. Mr. Browne chewed me out tonight because I messed up some of my songs and Mr. and Mrs. Davinci were there.

They were checking out Blue Moon to see if they want to hire us to play their party at the Dunes Club. I just hope I didn't foul up the deal."

"I hope not, too. I'm sorry that you're all tied up in emotional knots, but there is absolutely no excuse for letting your personal problems affect your friendship with Laurel or the future of the band." Mrs. Reynolds got up and went over to Denise, putting her hands on her daughter's shoulders. "Now call Laurel, wash that gunk off your face, and go to bed. And first thing tomorrow morning, I want you to get your head together and figure out how you're going to deal with the situation sensibly, calmly, and responsibly." Smiling slightly, she added, "You're not the first person in the world to discover that falling in love isn't all it's cracked up to be, you know."

"Who said I'm in love?" Denise protested feebly.

Her mother didn't say another word. She just bent down to kiss Denise's cheek, then left the room.

* * *

After Denise got ready for bed, she went downstairs to telephone Laurel. The minute Laurel answered, Denise began to grovel.

"Laurel, you can't see me but I'm on my hands and knees right now. I'm begging you to forgive me for ditching you tonight. It was a creepy thing to do, and I can't tell you how sorry I am. I'll apologize to your mother, too, if you want me to. Are we still friends?"

Laurel laughed. "I guess so. But what got into you, anyway? You shot off that stage like a rocket. What's going on? I'm assuming it has something to do with Joe Ormand. Am I right?"

"Well, yes." Taking a deep breath, Denise said, "I saw you and Joe talking and I freaked out. Then Cara showed up, and you all seemed so friendly that I thought you'd turned on me. I guess that was a little paranoid, but . . ." Denise's excuse petered out.

"Yeah, just a little! First of all, I was only talking to Joe because he approached *me* to find out what was wrong with *you*. I didn't know what to tell him. As for Miss Perfect Smithson, I hardly said more than a couple of words to her all evening. And secondly, after fifteen years of friendship, that's all the confidence you have in me? Gee, thanks a lot, Denise!"

"I know, I know," Denise said with a sigh. "I don't know what came over me."

"I do. Joe Ormand. You know, Denise, he really does seem like a nice guy, and I think he's genuinely confused about the way you're acting. Are you *positive* he and Cara are a couple?" Laurel asked.

"Oh, come on, Laurel. Wouldn't you say the weight of evidence is against them? They went together for almost a year, and now every time I turn around they're together again. Cara's perfectly gorgeous, and I'm a perfect goof. If you were Joe, who would *you* choose? Don't answer that," Denise added hastily. "Anyway, it doesn't really matter. I've had it up to here with this whole thing. I'll admit I'm crazy about Joe Ormand, but I'm not going to let him drive me any crazier. I've acted like too much of a lunatic as it is."

"So what happens next?" Laurel asked.

"Nothing. Not a single thing. I've got to get my life back on track—if I don't, I'll lose my job and my friends. From now on, I'm going to pretend that Joe Ormand doesn't exist. It's my only hope of surviving this summer."

"Well, okay. I guess you know what you're doing," Laurel said, but she sounded doubtful.

"I always know what I'm doing," Denise announced, then added a little wistfully, "or at least I used to." Giving herself a mental shake, she went on, "Now that's settled, let's plan something fun for tomorrow. Got any ideas?"

"It's supposed to rain," Laurel said, "so why don't you come over to my house? We can veg out, read magazines, watch soaps, stuff like that."

"Sounds great—just what the doctor ordered," Denise agreed with more enthusiasm than she felt. "See you in the morning. And Laurel?"

"What?"

"Thanks for still speaking to me, and for being my friend after the way I acted tonight."

Laughing, Laurel said, "Forget it, you dope. And if you want me to keep on being your friend, let me go to bed and get some sleep, okay?"

"Okay. 'Night."

Denise was smiling as she hung up the phone. *Tomorrow*, she thought. *Tomorrow is the new first day of summer.*

Chapter Eight

Denise had no trouble avoiding Joe for the next few days, thanks to a long stretch of rainy weather. She refused to answer the telephone when it rang, afraid she'd get caught in an awkward conversation with him if he called. Joe left several messages for her with Mark, asking Denise to call him back, but she didn't. After a while, he stopped phoning, and Denise almost succeeded in convincing herself that she was glad.

But the real test of her resolve came on the first sunny day. Though Denise got up extra early to finish her morning run before

Joe arrived, she knew she wouldn't be able to dodge him when she and Laurel went to the beach later on.

"Are you sure you're ready for this?" Laurel asked as they stood in a long line of sun-starved beach lovers, waiting to flash their passes at the guard by the pavilion gates.

"Why shouldn't I be?" Denise said. "I'm certainly not going to stay home for the rest of the summer just because of Joe Ormand. Believe me, Laurel, I know I can handle it."

A few minutes later, they joined their gang of friends in the usual place. After a quick dip in the ocean, during which Denise managed to avoid looking in the direction of the lifeguard tower where Joe generally sat, she lay down on her stomach next to Kevin while Laurel, Evan, and Marcia headed for the volleyball net much farther down the beach.

"You okay, Denise?" Kevin asked, glancing over at her.

Squinting at him suspiciously, Denise said, "Sure. Why?"

He grinned. "Well, to begin with, you didn't reorganize us the minute you got here—it's the first time all summer we haven't been 'Denised.' And how come you're lying here soaking up the rays instead of taking charge of the volleyball game?" He shook his head in mock concern. "That's not like you. What happened to your get-up-and-go?"

Denise closed her eyes. "Good question," she murmured, half to herself. "I guess my get-up-and-go just got up and went."

"Run that past me again?" Kevin said. "I could hardly hear you."

"Never mind," Denise sighed. "It wasn't really very important."

A short while later, as she started to roll over onto her back, Denise happened to glance casually down the beach. To her dismay, the tall, lanky figure of Joe Ormand was striding purposefully toward her. With a little gasp, Denise lay down flat and closed her eyes, hoping Joe would think she was asleep.

Joe didn't buy it. When he reached her blanket, he poked her gently in the ribs with one bare foot. There was no way Denise could pretend she didn't feel it, so she looked up at him.

"Oh, hi, Joe," she said, trying to sound surprised. "What's happening?"

"You tell me," Joe replied quietly. "We need to talk. Any chance I could convince you to take a little walk with me?"

"Yeah, Denise, take a walk," Kevin mumbled sleepily. "The exercise will do you good."

Denise sat up. "I don't know—I really ought to go get Laurel," she hedged. "I forgot to tell her that I wrangled us a free racquetball session at the health club this afternoon. . . ."

"Fine. We'll walk to the volleyball net then," Joe said. He stretched out his hand, and Denise reluctantly allowed him to pull her to her feet. He let go of her hand immediately as they walked side by side down to the hard-packed sand at the water's edge.

"Look, I really don't have time to talk now," Denise said, quickening her pace. "Why don't you give me a call later or something?"

"You mean, so I can leave another message and you can refuse to call me back? No way! I don't know what's bugging you, but I want to explain about something that happened the other night."

Denise walked even faster. "You mean, the

104

night of the jazz concert?" she said icily. "The one you said you were taking your mother to because I couldn't go?"

Joe matched his stride to hers. "Right. What I wanted to tell you is—"

"You don't have to tell me anything, Joe," Denise interrupted. "I really don't want to hear about you and Cara. Now if you don't mind, I've got to get to Laurel."

"I *do* mind!" Joe almost yelled. "Besides, I don't want to talk about Cara and me. I want to talk about *you* and me."

Denise started to run. "There *is* no you and me!" she said. "Good-bye, Joe. Have a nice life."

He didn't try to catch up with her. When Denise sneaked a quick peek over her shoulder, she saw him standing still, a bewildered look on his face. For a moment, she felt a sharp pang of regret, guilt, or apprehension— she wasn't sure which.

I did the right thing, she told herself as she jogged more slowly up the beach to where the volleyball game was still in progress. *Mom told me to deal with the situation sensibly, and that's exactly what I did.*

But a small, annoying voice in her head said, "Oh, yeah? Wouldn't it have been more sensible at least to hear him out? After all, he did say he wanted to talk about the two of you. Why didn't you wait to hear what he had to say?"

"Get real!" Denise muttered in reply. "What *could* he say that wouldn't humiliate me more than he's done already? I must have been out of my mind to think even for a minute that Joe could prefer gawky, loud-mouthed me to cuddly, adorable Cara. Now will you please just *shut up*?"

"Gee, Denise, I haven't said a word."

Denise realized that Laurel was standing next to her, looking very confused. Forcing a smile she said, "Sorry—I didn't mean you. I was just giving myself a talking-to."

She told Laurel about the racquetball session, and as they walked back to their blanket, Laurel said casually, "I happened to notice that you and Joe were having a conversation a few minutes ago—or maybe it was a race, I couldn't really tell. If it was a conversation, what did he have to say? And if it was a race, who won?"

Denise shrugged. "He really didn't have much of anything to say—nothing important, anyway." She gave a short, humorless laugh. "As for who won the race, Cara Smithson did, and she wasn't even there!"

Two nights after her encounter with Joe on the beach, Denise was doing her best to feel really good about herself and her summer again. In spite of her less than stellar performance at the state beach dance, Blue Moon had landed the Davinci party, and Denise was into her third song of the evening, belting out an upbeat number from *Kiss Me, Kate*. She was in a groove, and for once she knew she looked great in a fabulous purple off-the-shoulder cocktail dress she'd found at a rummage sale. Denise had been saving it for a special occasion, and performing at the swanky Dunes Club was definitely that.

Unlike the beach club where Denise and her friends spent most of their days, the Dunes Club was the most elegant in Green Hill Cove, or anywhere in the state, for that matter. Every member drove a fancy car, wore nothing but real jewelry, and didn't blink an eye at spending forty dollars for a lunch of tuna sandwiches and soda. The clubhouse itself was a sprawling Gothic-style structure that had once been the palatial home of a multimillionaire tycoon.

Denise couldn't help enjoying the glamorous, festive atmosphere. While the band played a few bars between verses of the song, Denise stood on the elaborate bandstand that had been set up on the clubhouse terrace overlooking the ocean, remembering the only other time she had been there.

She was in junior high, and one of the girls in her class had invited her to a birthday party at the Dunes Club. Denise had never been so nervous in her life—she was sure she'd trip over her own big feet, say the wrong thing, pick up the wrong fork, walk around with food stuck in her braces. She didn't really enjoy the party at all, and when it was over, she swore she'd never come back, not even if they paid her.

Funny how things had worked out—here she was, and they *were* paying her. Glancing off to the side of the bandstand, Denise saw

Mr. Browne grinning at her. Apparently he was pleased with her performance so far.

During her first break, Denise decided to wander around the place for a little while. The entire club had been lavishly decorated with a fifties theme, and there was even a pink mint-condition '57 Chevy convertible in the middle of the main lawn. Elegantly dressed little kids and a few equally elegant teenagers were taking turns piling in and pretending to drive, while Elvis records played over the public address system during Blue Moon's break.

Denise approached one of the many refreshment tables set up under the trees and asked the bartender for a cranberry juice. She had just started across the lawn, looking for an empty bench where she could sit and savor her drink, when two small boys marched up to her. They looked to be about seven or eight years old, and were identically dressed in navy blue brass-buttoned blazers and beige slacks, just like miniature tycoons.

Smiling down at them, Denise said, "Hi. Can I do something for you?"

"Yes," said the slightly taller of the two. Denise noticed that he was missing a front tooth. "You see, miss, the people who work here aren't supposed to eat or drink any of the refreshments," he told her very seriously. "They're only for invited guests."

"That's right," the other child added with a solemn nod.

A little taken aback, Denise said, "Really? I didn't know that. I was under the impression that Mr. and Mrs. Davinci wanted the band to help themselves to whatever they wanted—within reason, of course. At least, that's what we were told by our boss, Mr. Browne."

The two boys just looked at her. Neither of them cracked a smile. Denise was beginning to get a little annoyed, but reminding herself that they were only children after all, she said lightly, "Hey, what do you care? Who are you, anyway—the club detectives or something?" Turning to the taller one, she asked, "What's your name? Mine's Denise Reynolds."

"I'm Derrick Smithson," he announced. "It's a club rule about the hired help not

110

being allowed to have refreshments at a private party, and it's every member's responsibility to enforce the rules."

"That's right," the other kid said again with a smirk.

I don't believe this, Denise thought. *I simply do not believe it! This obnoxious little brat has to be Cara's brother. I should have known the Smithsons would belong to the Dunes Club! And I bet Cara's here, too, partying up a storm.*

Glancing around to see if anyone was within earshot, she saw only the bartender, who was busy emptying ice into a cooler. Bending down so her face was only inches away from Derrick's, Denise lowered her voice to just above a whisper. "Listen, you two little twerps, and listen good. Blue Moon is not 'hired help.' We happen to be the hottest band on the eastern seaboard, and the Dunes Club is lucky that we could fit this tacky little party into our busy schedule. Now unless you want me to dump this glass of cranberry juice right over your nasty little heads, I suggest you get lost *right now!*"

The boys' eyes were as big as quarters

111

when she had finished. They exchanged a panicked look and darted off across the lawn.

Denise was fuming. Stomping over to the table, she slammed her glass down on it without taking a single sip, and headed for the bandstand.

Five minutes later, she was back onstage, but she couldn't recapture her earlier good mood. Though she went through all the motions, Denise felt as if she were on automatic pilot, or a robot cleverly programmed to sing and dance. Nobody but Denise herself seemed to notice that she wasn't giving the performance her all, not even Mr. Browne.

After a couple of numbers, she was just beginning to hit her stride again when she glanced out at the dancing couples on the terrace. Cara was gliding past the bandstand in the arms of a sandy-haired boy, and Denise's heart gave a sickening lurch. Was it Joe? She was relieved when a closer look assured her it wasn't, but Cara looked disgustingly stunning in a ruffly white creation that put Denise's rummage-sale find to shame, and the boy was gazing down at her as if she were the only girl in the world. Denise felt a sharp pang of envy. Did Joe look at Cara like that when they were dancing? No boy had ever looked at *her* like that, that was for sure, and until she met Joe, it hadn't mattered. A tall, muscular, dark-haired guy cut in, and a moment later Cara and her new partner were lost in the crowd of dancers, but a moment was all it took to shatter Denise's fragile self-confidence. Feeling like a large, leggy weed in her forty-year-old dress, she could hardly wait for the set to be over.

By the time her second break came around, Denise was in no mood to hang out with the other band members. Besides, her throat was parched. Not wanting to have another encounter like her earlier episode with Cara's horrid little brother and his sidekick, she began searching for a water fountain. Having found one inside the clubhouse near the ladies' room, Denise drank her fill, then wandered down a carpeted hallway and through a set of French doors.

She found herself on another terrace, this one deserted except for a few elderly couples who appeared to be either enjoying the sunset or boycotting the Davincis' party. Denise crossed it and began walking aimlessly across a perfectly manicured lawn, too distressed by the mental comparison between herself and Cara to pay attention to where she was going. When she paused to get her bearings, Denise realized that she had walked all the way to the pool area. Though it was almost eight o'clock, a number of kids were still splashing and shouting in the water, supervised by a lone lifeguard who suddenly looked very familiar.

Joe saw her at the same moment Denise recognized him. Before she could turn away and beat a hasty retreat, he strode over to her, a puzzled expression on his freckled face.

"What are you doing here?" he asked.

Denise raised her chin defiantly. "I might ask you the same question."

Grinning, Joe said, "I'd think that was pretty obvious. I'm filling in for a pal of mine who was supposed to work the pool tonight. He got sick, so I volunteered to cover for him. But I'm willing to bet you're not planning on a quick dip, considering what you're wearing. You look terrific, Denise," he added. If Denise didn't know better, she would have sworn she saw genuine admiration in his hazel eyes. "I didn't know you were a member of the Dunes Club."

"I'm not," Denise told him emphatically. "I wouldn't join this club even if I could afford it, which I can't."

"Me either," Joe agreed. "Even those little monsters in the pool are pint-size snobs. So what *are* you doing here?"

"Blue Moon's playing for the Davincis' party up at the clubhouse," she said. "We're on a break, so I thought I'd take a walk, explore the place a little. I wound up here at the pool kind of by accident."

"Maybe not. Maybe it was fate," Joe said. "Remember what you said when you read my palm at the Chinese restaurant about my having a strong fate line?"

Though Denise remembered everything about that evening very well, she said coolly, "Did I? I must have been making it up—I don't know anything about reading palms."

Joe turned back to the pool to yell at a couple of kids who were trying to drown each other in the shallow end, then looked at Denise again. "Listen," he said seriously. "I get off duty at eight-thirty. I don't know how long your party's going to last, but I could hang around until it's over and maybe we could go somewhere for a while and talk. You owe me an explanation, you know."

"*I* owe *you* an explanation!" Denise exclaimed. "That's news to me! Anyway, I have to get home after the show. And besides, aren't you going to be pretty busy tonight?"

Joe looked confused. "Me? Why? What am I supposed to be doing?"

"How should I know?" Denise said. She couldn't prevent herself from adding, "But since Cara's at the party, I imagine that whatever it is, you'll be doing it with her."

"Well, you can stop imagining, because you're wrong." Joe sounded exasperated. "In the first place, I didn't know Cara was here, and in the second place, I don't care, okay?" He looked at her thoughtfully. "You know something? I think I'm beginning to get the picture about why you've been acting so weird lately. I've got to get back to work, and I guess you do, too. When you get home tonight, *call me.* Please?" he added, with a smile that Denise found almost impossible to resist.

"I—I might be kind of late . . ."

"I don't care how late it is. I don't care if it's three o'clock in the morning!" Joe declared. "I will be sitting by the phone, waiting for you to call, and if you don't, I will come to your house and bang on your front door and wake up your nice mother and your strange brother and your psychotic dog and all the neighbors and . . ."

Giggling, Denise said, "All right, all right! I'll call!"

"Great," Joe said with an approving nod. "Talk to you later."

He walked back to the pool, and Denise started off across the lawn. Checking her watch, she realized that if she didn't make tracks, she'd be late for the next set and Mr. Browne would be furious. She picked up her pace, stumbling a little in her high-heeled sandals. As she ran, Denise wondered if she was really running *to* the clubhouse, or *from* the prospect of a confrontation with Joe.

Chapter Nine

It was almost eleven o'clock when Denise drove home from the Dunes Club. The Davinci party was the longest gig Blue Moon had ever performed, and she was exhausted, but she also felt a surprising sense of accomplishment. Both Mr. and Mrs. Davinci had complimented the band in general, and Denise in particular, saying that Blue Moon had been largely responsible for the success of their party. They had even provided a sumptuous buffet supper for the band members after the final set—Denise had never eaten so much delicious lobster salad in her life, and she drank more than enough cranberry juice to make up for the glass she'd missed earlier.

During the last two sets she'd forced herself to shut both Joe and Cara out of her mind, concentrating only on the music and the routines Mr. Browne and the band had worked so hard to perfect. And it hadn't been easy, considering that Cara was the belle of the ball, dancing with one guy after another right under Denise's nose. As for Joe, she simply refused to think about what he might have to say when she called him—*if* she called him.

Now, however, as she pulled up to the curb in front of her house, her thoughts returned to Joe. Denise suspected that Cara had ditched him for the second time, and that the only reason he insisted on her phoning him tonight was because he was on the rebound. *Who does he think he is, anyway?* she asked herself, getting out of her bug. *Does he think he can drop me like a hot potato then pick me up again like—like a potato chip? Joe may be cute, but he's not that cute. I have my pride, after all!*

When Denise walked into the kitchen, her mother was sitting on a stool at the counter, having a cup of tea. Rather than asking how the performance went as she usually did, Mrs. Reynolds thrust a slip of paper at Denise.

"Joe called a few minutes ago," she said. "He said that you were supposed to call him, but he was afraid you'd change your mind. Does this mean that you haven't resolved the situation between the two of you?"

"Not exactly." Denise dropped a tea bag into a mug and turned the gas on under the kettle. She leaned down to pat Bibeau, who was leaping up and down, demanding attention. "I mean, we talked a little bit tonight and he asked me to call him when I got home so we could talk some more, but I don't see what good it would do."

Mrs. Reynolds sighed. "Denise, why are you doing this to yourself? Why won't you give Joe a chance? Why are you running away from a boy who genuinely seems to care about you?"

"Oh, sure!" Denise said angrily. "He cares about me so much that he sneaked off with another girl the minute my back was turned! Come on, Mom—you don't seriously expect me to welcome him back with open arms after that, do you?"

"Denise, I'm not trying to tell you what to do," her mother said wearily. "I'm just telling you that, since you are a decent, good-hearted person, you owe this boy the chance to explain himself. It won't kill you to pick up the phone just this once."

Denise groaned. "Okay, okay! I give up!" She snatched the note from her mother's hand. "I'll call him right now. Mind if I use the phone in your studio?"

"Be my guest," Mrs. Reynolds said cheerfully. "But before you do, I have a tidbit of gossip you might be interested in."

Rolling her eyes in exasperation, Denise said, "Mom, do you or don't you want me to make this call? Can't whatever it is wait until I'm off the phone?"

"I don't really think it can." Her mother had an odd expression on her face. "I think you should hear this *before* you call Joe."

Curious now, Denise folded her arms

across her chest and leaned against the door to the basement. "Okay, I'm waiting."

"You will never in a million years guess who your brother has been seeing," Mrs. Reynolds said, still smirking.

"This big news is about *Mark*?" Denise said incredulously. "No offense, Mom, but at the moment I couldn't care less who he's dating. I've got my own miserable romantic situation to deal with, remember?" She was about to go downstairs when her mother's words froze her in her tracks.

"What if I told you that Mark is seeing Cara Smithson, and that he was her date at the Davincis' party tonight?"

Denise spun around and stared at her. "You've got to be kidding!" she gasped. "That's not possible! If he'd been there I would have seen him!"

Grinning, her mother said, "I am not kidding, and it *is* possible. I was really surprised when you didn't mention seeing Mark, but you probably did and simply didn't recognize him. I hardly recognized my own son when he came downstairs this evening all duded up in a white dinner jacket, complete with boutonniere."

"I don't believe this!" Denise cried. "Come to think of it, I probably *did* see him dancing with Cara, but it didn't register." She sat down on the stool next to her mother. "When did you find out about Mark and Cara?" she asked eagerly. "*How* did you find out? Why didn't he tell me he was coming to the party?"

"You couldn't care less about who Mark's dating, huh?" Mrs. Reynolds said with a twinkle in her eye. "To answer your uninterested questions, I only found out tonight. Naturally enough, I asked your elegantly attired brother where he was off to, and he told me that a girl named Cara Smithson had invited him to escort her to the Davincis' party. He asked me if I knew Cara, and I said I knew *of* her, but I'd never met her. As to why he didn't mention it to you since he knew Blue Moon was performing, I haven't the slightest idea. You know your brother—he's not very big on sharing information."

"That's putting it mildly!" Denise shook her head in amazement.

"He did say something about wanting me to meet Cara, though," her mother continued. "Between you and me, I think Mark is smitten."

"This is so weird!" Denise said. "I can't even imagine how Mark and Cara would have met. It's not as if they run with the same crowd or anything."

"According to your brother, they met at the bowling alley one night a few weeks ago," her mother told her.

"The *bowling alley*?" Denise echoed. "Mother, Cara Smithson is *not* the kind of girl who goes to bowling alleys! You must have heard wrong."

"There's nothing wrong with my hearing," Mrs. Reynolds said. "Apparently Cara *does* go to bowling alleys. And I'll bet she goes to a lot of other 'normal' places, too, the way you and your friends do." Smiling, she added, "In fact, honey, did it ever occur to you that Cara might be an ordinary person who just happens to be extraordinarily pretty?"

Denise had to admit that it hadn't. While she was considering this possibility, her mother added, "Now that you know about

Cara and Mark, how about making that phone call? It seems pretty clear that Joe hadn't been dating Cara as you assumed, so I think you owe him an apology."

Leaping off the stool, Denise charged across the room and down the basement stairs. She skirted her mother's drawing board, sat down at the desk, and after taking a deep breath, dialed the number on the note.

Joe picked up in the middle of the first ring. When Denise identified herself, he said, "Hey, you really called! That's fantastic! I was just about to come over and carry out my threat to lay siege to your house."

"That's not such a bad idea," Denise said with a little laugh. "Not the yelling and banging part," she added, "just the coming over part. I think it would be better for us to talk in person, if that's okay with you."

There was dead silence on the other end of the line.

"Joe? Are you still there?" she asked anxiously.

"Yeah, I'm still here. Since you've been avoiding me like the plague, I'm just recovering from the shock. Be there in about ten minutes. And Denise?"

"Yes?"

"Promise me you won't say anything until I've finished, okay?"

"I promise," Denise said. "Or at least, I promise to try!"

When Joe's truck pulled up in front of her house, she was waiting at the curb. "No, don't get out," Denise said as he started to open the door. "I'm getting in." Sitting down beside him, she explained, "Mom's prowling around the house, so I thought we'd have more privacy out here. Not that she'd eavesdrop or anything, but . . ."

"Denise, you're babbling," Joe said gently. "My turn to talk, remember?"

She nodded and clasped her hands tightly in her lap.

"As far as I can tell, the problem between you and me is Cara Smithson," he began.

Before he could go on, Denise said eagerly, "Yes, but I just found out—"

"*Denise!* You promised!"

"Sorry," she mumbled. "I won't interrupt again, honest."

"Okay. Here is the story of Cara and me. As you know, we dated for about a year, and when she broke up with me, I was kind of bent out of shape. I mean, one day she was my girlfriend, and the next day she told me that she didn't want to see me anymore. Then when she immediately started dating Billy Keene, I felt like an old jalopy that's been traded in for a flashy new model."

I know that feeling well, Denise thought ruefully.

"So I swore off girls for months," Joe continued. "I wasn't interested in anyone at all— until I met you that day on the beach. Suddenly everything was terrific! I liked you a lot, you seemed to like me, we had a great time on our date, and then boom! It's over, just like that, and I'm starting to wonder what's wrong with me, why girls keep ditching me."

"Oh, Joe," Denise murmured, touching his arm. She had to bite her lip to stop herself from saying anything else.

"With a little detective work, plus some input from Laurel, I have now managed to figure out what happened. Laurel told me you saw me at the jazz concert with Cara, so you probably assumed I'd lied to you about taking my mom, and that Cara and I were back together, right? Just nod or shake your head," he added quickly.

Denise nodded.

"Wrong," Joe said. "I phoned Mom like I said I was going to, but before I could ask her about the concert, she told me that Cara had just called wanting to talk to me and she sounded really upset. So I called her back, and it turned out that Billy Keene had just broken up with her. I don't think anyone has ever broken up with Cara before—she was really wrecked, and I felt sorry for her. That's *all* I felt, Denise, just sorry.

"I don't know if you've noticed, but Cara doesn't have any close friends. She needed a shoulder to cry on, and somebody to cheer her up, so I asked her to go with me to the concert. She came, she talked, I listened, and for the life of me I couldn't remember why I'd been so crazy about her. I mean, Cara's a perfectly nice girl and everything but—well, she's no you."

Denise's heart was pounding so hard and fast that she actually felt a little dizzy. It sounded as if Joe *did* care about her, and that he really had gotten over Cara. But there was one more thing she needed to know, whether he was finished or not.

"So what were you two doing at the state beach dance?" she asked.

"We weren't there together," Joe said. "I went stag because I wanted to catch your gig, maybe even see you alone for a few minutes to try to discover why you were freezing me out. I guess Cara went by herself, too—I ran into her, and she talked my ear off about some college guy she'd met, as if she'd forgotten all about Billy Keene."

"That college guy is my brother Mark," Denise told him. "That's what I started to tell you before—I just found out tonight that while I thought you were seeing Cara, she was seeing Mark. Oh, Joe, I've been acting like such a jerk! I wouldn't blame you if you never wanted to speak to me again."

Chuckling softly, Joe put his arm around her. "Are you kidding? I'm just glad that you're finally speaking to *me*." In the faint light cast by a nearby streetlamp, he looked down at Denise. "Now I've got a proposition for you. Suppose we start all over, as if none of this nonsense ever happened. Do you think you could give me a second chance?"

Denise stared at him, wide-eyed. "You can't be serious! You really want to go out with me again after the mess I made of everything?"

Joe grinned. "Guess I'm just a glutton for punishment. So what do you say? Can we give it another try?"

"Well, if you're really, really sure . . ."

He pulled her closer. "Yes, Denise, I am really, really sure. I'll pick you up Thursday night around eight-thirty. And don't have supper—we'll grab a bite to eat somewhere, okay?"

Denise raised her face to his, answering him by her warm response to his gentle kiss.

When Denise floated back into the house a few minutes later, her mother called down from the second floor, "Well? What happened?"

With a dreamy smile on her face, Denise drifted up the stairs. "Nothing. Everything."

Her mother followed her to her room and sat down on the bed. "Would you care to be a little more specific, dear?"

Denise kicked off her sandals and began wiggling out of her dress. "Okay. In a nutshell, Joe explained and I apologized."

"That's it?" Mrs. Reynolds asked incredulously.

"Well, not quite. There are just one or two more minor details . . ." Grinning from ear to ear, Denise hugged herself. "He kissed me and we're going out Thursday night!"

Her mother beamed. "Oh, honey, that's wonderful!" She added, "And to think all this misery you've been going through could have been avoided if you'd just listened to the boy in the first place."

"I know," Denise said sheepishly. She sat down on the bed beside her mother. "I guess I was too afraid of what I was going to hear. I didn't think I could compete with Cara, so I just dropped out of the race."

"That's not the way I brought you up," Mrs. Reynolds said, shaking her head. "You've never been a quitter, Denise. But as I think I mentioned some time ago, it's hard to think straight when you're in love."

Denise pretended to scowl at her. "Love? Who's in love?" Then, giggling, she threw her arms around her mother and gave her a huge hug. "Me, that's who!" Suddenly she sobered. "Oh, Mom, I think I really *am* in love with Joe," she whispered. "It's kind of scary. What if he doesn't feel the same way about me?"

Mrs. Reynolds stroked her hair. "I may be just a little bit prejudiced, but in my opinion he'd have to be crazy *not* to." She kissed Denise's forehead and said right before she left the room, "Now get ready for bed, dear. Tomorrow's a whole new day."

A whole new day, Denise thought. *Maybe my perfect summer is finally going to begin for real!*

On Thursday night, Denise took one last look in the hall mirror before running out to Joe's waiting truck. Since he hadn't told her

133

where they were going or what they were going to do, she'd decided on a casual look—jeans, a white tank top, a purple cotton sweater tossed over her shoulders, and matching purple espadrilles on her feet. Her eyes were sparkling, her tanned skin glowed, and for once, Denise was almost satisfied with her appearance.

The sun had set and twilight was closing in as she got into Joe's pickup and fastened her seat belt. He looked at her with a goofy smile on his face. "Hi," he said, leaning over and lightly kissing her cheek.

Denise blushed. "Hi yourself." They sat for a moment in silence, gazing into each other's eyes. Denise spoke first. "So where are we going?"

Grinning, Joe said, "That's for me to know and you to find out. Close your eyes, and keep them closed until we get there."

"Why? So I can't find my way home if you dump me somewhere?" Denise teased.

"Is that the kind of guy you think I am? I'll have you know I have never dumped anybody anywhere. Now will you please shut your eyes?"

Denise did. Joe drove for what seemed to her like forever, though it couldn't have been more than ten or fifteen minutes. When he finally came to a stop and turned off the ignition, they'd made so many twists and turns that Denise had completely lost her bearings.

"Okay—you can open them now," Joe said.

She looked around, and was amazed to discover that they were parked next to the Town Green only a few blocks away from her house.

"Revisiting the scene of the crime, huh?" Denise said wryly.

"Since we're starting all over, I thought this would be a good place to begin," Joe replied as they got out of the pickup. "Just hang out while I get everything ready."

Denise watched with interest while he hauled an armload of stuff out of the back of the truck, then followed him across the green to a secluded spot beneath some tall trees.

Joe spread a plaid blanket on the grass and set a huge picnic basket next to it. Opening the basket, he took out two china plates, two crystal goblets, silverware, cloth napkins, and finally the most tempting array of picnic food Denise had ever seen.

The moon was beginning to rise by the time Joe had arranged everything to his satisfaction. Then he turned on two small flashlights and set them on end like candles. Finally he placed a tape player on top of the basket. A moment later, sweet, soft jazz began to play. With an elaborate wave of his hand, he motioned for Denise to be seated, then ceremoniously opened a bottle of ginger ale, filled the goblets, and handed one to her.

Sitting down next to her, Joe raised his glass. "I'd like to propose a toast," he said softly. "To new beginnings, and to a very special girl."

"Oh, Joe," Denise murmured as he touched his goblet to hers. "Thank you, but I'm not really special. I'm just . . ."

Joe took her glass and placed it next to his on the blanket. "Listen to what I am about to say and repeat after me: I am beautiful."

Denise felt her cheeks flaming. "Joe, this is silly. I'm not—"

"Repeat after me," Joe ordered sternly.

"I am—beautiful," she whispered.

"I am wonderful."

"I am wonderful."

"And Joe loves me."

Denise caught her breath. "Do you—do you really mean that?"

Smiling, Joe nodded and said again, "Repeat after me."

Gazing into his eyes, Denise said in wonderment, "And Joe loves me." Just before she melted into his arms, she added very softly, "And I love him, too."

We hope you enjoyed reading this book. If you would like to receive further information about available titles in the Bantam series, just write to the following address, with your name and address: Kim Prior, Bantam Books, 61–63 Uxbridge Road, Ealing, London W5 5SA.

If you live in Australia or New Zealand and would like more information about the series, please write to:

Sally Porter
Transworld Publishers
(Australia) Pty Ltd
15–25 Helles Avenue
Moorebank
NSW 2170
AUSTRALIA

Kiri Martin
Transworld Publishers (NZ) Ltd
3 William Pickering Drive
Albany
Auckland
NEW ZEALAND

All Bantam and Young Adult books are available at your bookshop or newsagent, or can be ordered from the following address:
Corgi/Bantam Books, Cash Sales Department, PO Box 11, Falmouth, Cornwall TR10 9EN.

Please list the title(s) you would like, and send together with a cheque or postal order to cover the cost of the book(s) plus postage and packing charges of £1.00 for one book, £1.50 for two books, and an additional 30p for each subsequent book ordered to a maximum of £3.00 for seven or more books.

(The above applies only to readers in the UK, and BFPO)

Overseas customers (including Eire), please allow £2.00 for postage and packing for the first book, an additional £1.00 for a second book, and 50p for each subsequent title ordered.